DISASTER
ON
WINDY HILL

Adventures
of the Northwoods

DISASTER
ON
WINDY HILL

Lois Walfrid Johnson

BETHANY HOUSE PUBLISHERS
MINNEAPOLIS, MINNESOTA 55438

Big Gust Anderson, Charlie Saunders, and Walfrid Johnson lived in
the Grantsburg area in the early 1900s. Jim Frawley was gatekeeper
at Nevers Dam. Robert Lang was the construction supervisor who
designed the Lang gate. Originally Charles Nevers owned the
northwest Wisconsin farm where the dam was built. All other
characters in this book are fictitious. Any resemblance to persons
living or dead is coincidental.

Scripture quotations are from the 1901 American Standard edition of
the Revised Version of the Bible.

Cover illustration by Andrea Jorgenson.

Published by Bethany House Publishers
A Ministry of Bethany Fellowship, Inc.
11300 Hampshire Avenue South
Minneapolis, Minnesota 55438

Printed in the United States of America

Library of Congress Cataloging-in-Publication Data

Johnson, Lois Walfrid.
    Disaster at Windy Hill / Lois Walfrid Johnson.
        p. cm. — (Adventures of the northwoods ; bk. 10)
    Summary: After Kate buys Windsong and Breeza, two horses
with a mysterious past, someone sets the Nordstrom barn on fire and
Windsong disappears.

    [1. Swedish Americans—Fiction. 2. Christian life—Fiction.
3. Horses—Fiction. 4. Wisconsin—Fiction. 5. Mystery and
detective stories.] I. Title. II. Series: Johnson, Lois Walfrid.
Adventures of the northwoods ; 10.
PZ7.J63255Dis   1994
[Fic]—dc20   94–25694
ISBN 1–55661–242–7   CIP

To Diane,
Randy, and Renee,

because this is home,

and
with special love to Jessica

LOIS WALFRID JOHNSON is the bestselling author of more than twenty books. These include *You're Worth More Than You Think!* and other Gold Medallion winners in the LET'S-TALK-ABOUT-IT STORIES FOR KIDS series about making choices. Novels in the ADVENTURES OF THE NORTHWOODS series have received awards from Excellence in Media, the Wisconsin State Historical Society, and the Council for Wisconsin Writers.

Lois has a great interest in historical mystery novels, as you may be able to tell! She and her husband, Roy, are the parents of a blended family and live in rural Wisconsin.

Contents

1

Fire!

$\mathcal{F}$rom the beginning Katherine O'Connell had known it was going to be an extra special day. "I can hardly wait!" she exclaimed. "I'm going to buy the best horse in the whole world!"

As she jumped down from the farm wagon, Papa Nordstrom drove on. Kate headed toward Charlie Saunders' large stable. Her stepbrother Anders and their friend Erik Lundgren followed.

For the one hundredth time Kate pushed a hand deep into her pocket. The silver dollars clanked against each other, still safely there.

"I want a black horse," Kate said. "A black horse with a white blaze!"

Anders laughed. "Kate, you have to see what Charlie has for sale. You can't just name a color and buy according to that."

But Kate paid no attention. "You just wait. I'll find exactly the horse I want!"

Near the door leading into the livery stable a large poster caught her attention:

WARNING
EXTREMELY DRY CONDITIONS
CLEAR ALL WEEDS, TALL GRASS, AND BRUSH
AWAY FROM BUILDINGS

Kate stared at the words. All the way to town the fields had been unusually dry. Any reminder of what that could mean made Kate uneasy.

"Did you see that?" she asked the boys, nodding toward the sign.

Anders nodded grimly. "I don't like to think what would happen if our woods caught fire."

Pushing aside her worry, Kate pulled open the stable door. Along the wall hung harnesses and saddles. Standing among them was Charlie Saunders himself, the Burnett County sheriff and owner of the stable.

"We're here to look for a horse," Anders said quickly, as though afraid that Kate would say the wrong thing.

Charlie stroked his big handlebar mustache. "For you, Anders?"

Kate's tall blond brother shook his head. "For Kate, sir."

Charlie's grin told Kate that he remembered them because of the mystery they'd solved a few months before. "I've got just the horse for a spunky girl like you," he said, leading them toward the stalls.

The stable was full, and Kate guessed there were more than sixty horses there. As they passed one horse after another, she looked at each one carefully. Many were owned by people who left their horses while shopping in Grantsburg. In that August of 1907 Charlie also rented out horses to people who needed them.

But Charlie offered something even more exciting. Now and then he bought a railroad car full of broncos—wild horses from out west. Maybe he'd have a spirited black one she could buy!

As they reached the last stall, Kate stopped. There was

a black horse, all right. Even in the dimness of the stable its coat was shiny.

"How about this one?" Kate called to Charlie as he walked on with the boys.

Charlie shook his head. "That's not the one I had in mind."

"Is he for sale?" Kate asked quickly.

"Prince? Sure," Charlie answered. "But he's—"

"Can I see him please?"

Anders stepped back, looked at the horse. "Kate, he's not for you."

Kate looked past her brother to Charlie. "Please?" she asked.

Charlie glanced at Anders, then back to Kate. "How much have you ridden?" he asked her.

"Oh, a lot," Kate said quickly. "I've been riding Wildfire, my brother's horse."

"Aw, Kate—" Anders started. "You haven't ridden that much."

But Kate stood there, waiting. Charlie went into the stall, snapped a lead rope onto Prince's halter, then led him out. Prince tossed his head, fighting the rope, and pranced sideways.

Charlie hung on, speaking sharply. "Settle down now."

With long thin legs, the horse looked like the royalty for which he was named. But when Charlie reached the door, Prince bolted through, trying to break away.

Charlie stood his ground. Outside, he unsnapped the rope and let the horse run in the fenced-in yard. Kate and the boys waited near the door, watching every movement. Prince trotted around the fifty- or sixty-foot area, his head high and tail flying.

"Isn't he a great horse?" Kate asked.

"Nope!" Erik spoke for the first time since they'd entered the livery stable. Like Anders, Erik was over six feet tall and broad shouldered from farm work. But Erik's hair was wavy and brown, while Anders had a thatch of blond hair that fell this way and that.

"What do you mean, *nope*?" Kate asked.

Anders turned around. "He's too much horse for you!"

"Too much horse!" Kate sputtered. "That's the one I want!"

Anders snorted.

"Ever since you bought Wildfire, I've wanted a black horse just like her."

"I hate to tell you, my dear sister. This is not a horse just like Wildfire. It's a stallion!"

When Charlie reached out for Prince's halter, the stallion backed off, his eyes rolling. On the second try Charlie caught him, but Prince flung his head, trying to get away. Charlie snapped on the lead rope and led him back into the stable.

"I can ride him, even if he is a stallion," Kate told Anders.

Anders shook his head. "No, you can't!"

"It's *my* money!" While in Michigan's Upper Peninsula, Kate had received the silver dollars as a reward. She loved the feel of making her own choice.

Again Kate reached inside her pocket. "I'll do what I want!" She started after Charlie.

Behind Kate, Anders groaned. "Sisters! I don't know how they can be so stupid!"

"That's the worst I've ever seen Kate act!" Erik sounded disappointed. "I can't think of a more awful choice than a wild stallion."

A warm flush of embarrassment flooded Kate's face. Just inside the stable, where the boys couldn't see her, she stopped. It was bad enough having Anders tell her what to do. A year and a half before, his father had married Kate's mother. Mama and Kate had moved from Minneapolis to northwest Wisconsin. Now Erik was their neighbor and special friend. Kate didn't want him to think she wasn't worth knowing.

For another minute she waited, listening. When Erik said no more, Kate tried to shrug it off. "Phooey on them!" she muttered. "Just because they're boys, they think they know everything!"

The dim stable seemed a cool contrast to the August sun. As though she were still seeing the dry fields on the way into town, Kate felt their heat. A strange thought entered her mind. *If we don't stick together as a family, we won't make it.*

Kate pushed the idea away. Ever since becoming a family they had worked together. Why should it be any different now? But the thought remained, like a cocklebur clinging to her clothing.

As Kate caught up with Charlie, Papa Nordstrom came through the door. Charlie tipped his head toward Kate.

"She's interested in this horse," he said evenly. Charlie kept walking toward the stall.

Papa took one glance at Prince, then turned to Kate. "What did Anders say?"

"Well—" Kate didn't want to tell him.

Papa looked back at Prince. "Anders is a good judge of horses. He didn't think it was the right one, did he?"

As Charlie led the stallion into his stall, Prince reared up on his hind legs. When he landed on the ground, Charlie quickly tied the lead rope to a ring. Staying clear of the rear hoofs, Charlie backed out of the stall.

Watching Prince, Kate felt uneasy, yet she hated to give in. "I want a spirited horse," she said. "Not some old nag."

"But Anders is right," Papa answered. "That stallion is too much horse for you."

"He's exactly what I've always wanted!" Kate wailed. "A spirited black horse!"

Papa looked at her, a warning in his eyes.

Kate closed her mouth, but her angry thoughts tumbled on. *You're just agreeing with Anders because he's your son!* she wanted to say.

Just in time Kate held back the words. If she were disrespectful, Papa would walk out. She would have no horse at all. It made no difference that she had her own money.

"It's a spirited horse you want?" Charlie asked Kate.

Kate nodded, her gaze still on Prince.

"Then I've got something you might like. He's not black, but he's spirited."

Charlie led Kate and Papa outside to where Anders and Erik sat on the top rail of the fence. Across the yard a pale gold horse stood near the water tank. Each time he moved, his muscles seemed to ripple in the sunlight.

Kate's heart leaped. It was a spirited horse, all right, but not in the same wild way as the stallion.

Charlie caught the halter and led the horse toward Papa and Kate. Papa's gaze followed every step.

"He'd give you a good ride," Papa told Kate as Charlie turned and walked the horse away in a straight line.

Kate watched with growing interest, but then Charlie reached the far side of the pen. Two other horses stood there. Even from where Kate stood, they seemed to be in poor condition. The rest of Charlie's horses looked so good that it made Kate curious.

Leaving the boys behind, she hurried across the fenced area. One of the horses was a black mare. The other was chestnut colored. Their coats looked rough and dry, as though no one had groomed them for months.

The mare looked especially shabby. Kate's throat tightened just seeing her. "Where did you get these horses?" she asked Charlie.

"From a man who used to work at Nevers Dam. Said he needed the money."

"Nevers?" Kate asked. "That's where my uncle Ben works. I wonder if they know each other."

On the St. Croix River, ten miles above the twin villages of St. Croix Falls, Wisconsin, and Taylors Falls, Minnesota, Nevers was known as the lumberman's dam. It controlled the water level for logs sent down the river to sawmills in Stillwater.

As Kate stood there, the mare edged close and nuzzled

her shoulder. The horse seemed friendly enough, but every rib showed.

Reaching out, Kate stroked the mare's shaggy back. She felt angry at an owner who would mistreat a horse in this way. When she and Charlie returned to the others, the mare followed Kate.

Anders grinned. "Mary had a little lamb!" he called.

Kate put a protective hand on the horse's neck. "She needs some good care!"

"That she does," Charlie answered.

The chestnut had followed the mare. His deep reddish brown coat also looked dull and without life. Though this was August, neither he nor the mare had shed their winter hair.

As she watched them, tears welled up in Kate's eyes. Hadn't anyone groomed the horses for months? What kind of food were they getting?

Hoping that no one had seen her tears, Kate blinked them away. But Papa had noticed.

"You can't buy a horse just because you feel sorry for it," he said gently. "It has to be the right one for you."

Kate nodded. "I know. But maybe the right one is an animal that needs a good home."

"The horses had the same owner," Charlie explained to Papa. "They stick together like fleas on a dog's back."

"They've both been neglected," Papa said.

After all her ideas about having a horse with a sleek coat, it no longer mattered to Kate. She just wanted to bring the mare back to good health.

"Can I ride the black mare?" she asked suddenly.

Anders stared at Kate. "You're interested in *this* horse?"

Kate nodded. "She likes me."

"Crazy girl!" Anders shook his head. "You sure jump from one kind of animal to another!"

Kate raised her chin. "I can change my mind," she said. "That's a woman's right."

"You're a girl, not a woman!" Anders scowled.

"What's the mare's name?" Kate asked Charlie.

"Windsong," he said.

"Windsong?" Kate felt surprised. It was a beautiful name, a strange contrast to the horse's appearance. Maybe the original owner had really loved her. Maybe the mare would ride like the wind.

Papa stood back, studying how the horse was built. "Let Anders try her first," he told Kate.

Anders jumped on, walked the mare around the fenced-in area, then urged her into a trot. When Charlie opened the large gate, Anders rode into the street.

Kate, Papa, and Erik followed him. As they turned toward the Hickerson Mill, Kate caught a quick movement out of the corner of her eye. Whirling around, she saw a hay wagon close to the stable. The large draft horses hitched to the wagon stood alone, as though waiting for the driver to return.

As Kate turned toward Anders once more, Windsong started to canter. Kate and the others walked behind until Anders rounded a bend in the road.

"Windsong moves well," Papa said, but Kate knew he was holding back his opinion.

Just then a shout rang out. "Fire!"

Kate spun around.

From near the stable a man shouted again. "Fire!"

A plume of smoke rose from the wagon. Greedy flames licked at the hay.

Kate broke into a run. Already the flames leaped upward to the open door of the loft.

2

Surprise Moves

*W*hen Kate reached the gate, Papa and Erik were right behind. Just then Charlie rushed out of the stable. While Papa held the terrified horses, Charlie and Erik unhitched them from the wagon.

"Buckets!" Kate cried, and Charlie ran back into the stable.

As Kate started to open the gate, the horses whinnied their fear. Just in time, Kate closed the gate again. If the horses broke out, they would race through the streets of Grantsburg.

Grabbing hold of the boards, Kate climbed the fence. As she dropped down on the other side, the fire bell began to ring.

By the time Kate reached the trough for watering horses, Charlie was there with buckets. Kate dipped them into the large tank, filling them with water. Charlie raced across the yard and handed them over the fence.

The hay wagon was burning now, its wooden cross-pieces a skeleton of flame. Kate's stomach knotted with fear.

If the stable caught fire, how would they ever get all those horses out?

Then Kate saw a very tall man striding along the street. Big Gust!

Instead of taking the time to hitch up horses, the seven-foot, six-inch village marshall pulled the fire wagon himself. In great long strides he hurried toward the fire. Other men ran alongside, trying to keep up.

At the burning hay wagon Big Gust stopped. Quickly men pulled hose from both ends of the pump wagon. One of the men raced toward the fence, slipped the hose through, and dropped the end into the water tank.

Big Gust grabbed the other end of the hose. Men lined up on both sides of the wagon. Up, down, up, down they pumped the barlike handles. As they worked in steady rhythm, water spurted from the end of the hose.

Big Gust held the hose high, spraying water across the side of the stable. As the men kept pumping, Gust wet down the boards. Then he turned the water onto the hay wagon.

By now, little was left of it. Gust flooded the charred boards, soaking every ember.

"That could have been a bad one," Charlie said when the fire was out. "I hate to think what might have happened to my horses."

Big Gust took out a large handkerchief and wiped the sweat from his forehead. Nearby, another fireman emptied a bucket of water over his head.

"Who started the fire?" Charlie asked. "Did any of you see someone hanging around?"

Kate thought back. Only minutes before, she had passed the wagon. She remembered how she had sensed a quick movement. Yet she hadn't seen anyone lurking around.

Standing back, Kate stared at the front of the stable, then at what was left of the hay wagon.

"We were walking away," she told Charlie. "Our backs were turned to the wagon. But it would take only a minute for someone to come around that corner."

"Or walk along the road," Erik said. "All he'd have to do is throw a match in the hay."

"Has anyone got it in for you?" Papa asked Charlie.

"Well, I don't know—" Charlie stroked his handlebar mustache, as though not wanting to think about revenge. Yet his eyes looked thoughtful. Was he wondering about each person he had ever arrested?

When Big Gust and the other firefighters left, Charlie shrugged. "Whoever set that fire is gone by now. You want to buy a horse, Kate. Let's get back to finding the right one."

During the fire Anders had returned with the black mare. Now Charlie brought out a small saddle and slung it over Windsong's back.

"She'll fatten up in no time," Charlie promised. "She just needs better feed."

"Could we give her extra oats?" Kate asked Papa.

"Yah," he answered after a moment of thought. "We'll do our best."

As Kate dropped into the saddle, Papa stepped close. "Take it easy till you know how she acts," he warned. "When an animal has been mistreated, you don't know what it'll do."

Leaning forward, Kate clucked to Windsong. The mare's ears turned to the sound of her voice. At first Kate walked her around the pen. Each time she asked the horse to do something, Windsong responded.

Erik swung up on Breeza, the chestnut horse, and also rode around the fenced-in area. Charlie opened the gate, and Kate took the mare into the street. When Erik followed, Kate remembered what he had said—*"That's the worst I've ever seen Kate act!"*

Suddenly she felt ashamed. She wished she could take back her angry words. *I'll prove to Erik that I'm someone he admires—someone my family feels proud of!*

Kate urged the mare into a canter. Halfway to the Hickerson Mill, she realized something. *This could be my horse— my very own horse!*

As Erik caught up, Breeza stayed even with Windsong. Erik grinned at Kate. It was easy to see that he was enjoying himself.

When Kate and Erik returned to the stable, Papa was talking to Charlie. "I want to make sure Kate gets a safe horse," he said. "A horse that won't buck her off."

"I rode both Windsong and Breeza myself," Charlie answered. "I didn't pick up a problem. I think the horses had a good owner before the last one."

When Kate slid to the ground, Papa opened Windsong's mouth, looked at her teeth, and picked up each foot. "Couple of shoes are loose," he told Charlie. "And the hooves need trimming."

"I know," Charlie answered. "I'll figure the cost of a blacksmith's work into your price."

When Charlie named the amount he wanted, Kate felt relieved. She had plenty of silver dollars. She could even buy something else for herself.

"Are you sure this is the horse for you?" Papa asked Kate. "If you take Windsong, you'll have to work hard to get her in shape. Can you handle it?"

Kate nodded.

"You can still choose that pale gold horse."

Kate knew that's what Papa hoped, but she shook her head.

"Then there's one condition," he answered. "If the mare doesn't behave, she comes back to Charlie. It's the only way you can take her."

Again Kate agreed. She felt sure she could turn Windsong into a good horse.

Papa turned to Charlie. "If she acts up and isn't safe to have around, I'll bring her back. All right?"

"Yup," Charlie answered.

Windsong had stayed nearby. Reaching up, Kate pushed

the forelock out of the mare's eyes. Her black coat seemed as dry as the land.

"You don't have a white blaze like I wanted," she said. "And you look really awful." Kate stroked the horse between her eyes. "But you'll help me, won't you?"

As though answering, the mare nodded.

Kate giggled. "She seems to understand! But how can she possibly know what I'm saying?"

Excitement stirred within Kate. Then she glanced toward Erik. He was smoothing Breeza's mane, as though he hated to say goodbye.

An idea popped into Kate's head. She turned back to Papa. "If we had both horses, could you use them as a team?"

Papa looked at Kate oddly. Standing back, he studied the two horses, then had them walk together. "They wouldn't be a matched pair, but they have the same gait."

"How much for the two of them?" Kate asked Charlie.

"If you want both, I'll give you a special deal. And I'll throw in some used saddles. A lighter one for you, so it's easier to lift." Again Charlie named his price.

Kate took one more look at the horses. She couldn't bear the idea of either one going to another terrible owner.

"Sold!" she said.

"*Sold?*" Anders asked. "Are you serious?"

"Yup!" Kate grinned. "It's my money!" She glanced toward Papa. "All right?"

He nodded. "All right."

"What on earth are you going to do with *two* horses?" Anders was still puzzled.

Lifting her head, Kate flipped her long black braid over her shoulder. "If Papa needs them, he can have a team."

She looked toward Erik to watch his expression. "And if Erik wants, he can ride Breeza."

Erik stared at her. "No big fancy horse? No wild stallion?"

Kate shook her head, relieved that the choice was made.

A wide grin spread across his face. "Thanks, Kate!" Erik exclaimed. "Thanks very much!"

Anders clapped him on the back. "Now we can all ride together!"

When the horses were saddled and ready, Kate and Erik rode out of the fenced-in area. Anders walked alongside.

Erik turned to Kate. "I can't believe that you managed to buy two horses!"

A warm spot glowed in Kate's heart, just hearing how Erik felt. *Maybe he doesn't think I'm so awful after all.* She knew how unusual it was for a young person to own a horse. In all of northwest Wisconsin she didn't know another girl who owned one horse, let alone two.

"Even though I had the money, it wasn't really mine." Kate wanted to change Erik's earlier opinion about her. "We all worked together to help my cousin in Michigan."

"Just the same, thanks a lot!" Erik answered.

"I want to do everything I can to take care of Windsong," Kate said.

Erik felt the same way about Breeza. "We'll have their coats shining in no time."

Walfrid Johnson's blacksmith shop was farther along the main street of Grantsburg. Papa had agreed to meet them there as soon as he bought what he needed at the feed store.

When Kate and the others reached the blacksmith shop, Stretch was working outside where it was cooler. Nearly a year before, the tall boy had attended Spirit Lake School. After dropping out, Stretch had smashed his hand between two large blocks of ice.

When he saw Kate, a glad light filled his eyes. "This is your horse?" he asked.

In spite of Windsong's appearance, Kate suddenly felt proud of her. "The other one is mine, too." She nodded toward Breeza. "But I'll ride Windsong most of the time."

One by one, Stretch lifted the mare's hooves, looking them over. "I'll have her fixed up in a jiffy."

Holding a front hoof between his knees, Stretch pulled

out the loose nails and removed the shoe.

"Your hand!" Kate exclaimed as Stretch trimmed the hoof. "Is it all right now?"

Stretch held out his injured hand for Kate to see. After his accident, three fingers had curled back toward the wrist. By now, two of the fingers had straightened out. The third was almost in the right position. Once again Stretch could use the hand as needed.

He was fitting a shoe on Windsong when a young man walked up. In spite of the heat, he wore a neatly buttoned shirt. A narrow neck scarf in the newest style—what some people called a necktie—hung down to his waist.

When the man walked close to the horses, Breeza became restless. Snorting loudly, he stamped his foot on the ground.

Windsong tossed her head. Suddenly she jerked her hoof away from Stretch. Her ears went back, flat against her head, as if she were ready to kick.

3

Ambush!

As she saw the whites of Windsong's eyes, Kate shuddered. Moving quickly, Erik grabbed Breeza's halter.

"Whoa there!" he commanded. "Settle down!"

Her heart in her throat, Kate backed away. "What did I buy?" she asked the boys. "Do I have a couple of wild horses?"

Stretch glanced toward the man who had just arrived. "They'll be fine," he told Kate. "Just treat 'em right."

As the young man circled around Stretch, he stayed clear of the two horses. "They're yours?" he asked Kate.

"My very own!" Again Kate felt the pride of ownership. "I just bought them."

"You live close by?" His voice sounded lazy, as if just making conversation.

Kate shook her head. "Eleven miles from here."

The man took out a cigar, then a match. "Which way?" he asked.

"Down near Trade Lake," Kate told him. "On Windy Hill Farm."

The minute she spoke Kate felt uneasy. Mama had told her never to talk to strangers. But this one was so handsome and well dressed, how could it possibly matter? Besides, Anders, Erik, and Stretch were right there.

The man lit the cigar, then waved the match to make it go out.

"Hey, watch what you're doing!" Stretch warned. "We've already had one fire in town today."

The man dropped the match, then ground it into the dirt. "You have a long way home, with rivers and all," he said to Kate.

"It's not bad," she answered. "We drop south, then go east. I like the ride into town."

Kate looked over to where Stretch was again shoeing the mare. "Now I can ride Windsong. I'll have her looking good in no time. The last person who owned her didn't take care of her."

"That so?" A strange look flashed across the man's face.

Kate wondered about it. What was it? Resentment? She wasn't sure. Whatever the look meant, it was already gone.

Once again Stretch picked up Windsong's hoof. As he nailed on a shoe, Stretch looked over to the man. "Can I help you with something?"

"I'll come back when you aren't busy," the man answered. Turning to Kate, he reached up, as though to lift a hat. "Well, good luck with your horses!" Taking a wide route around Windsong and Breeza, he reached the street.

Stretch was still working on Windsong when Papa arrived.

"I need to get back to the farm," he told Kate. "And Stretch needs time to shoe Breeza. Do you and Erik want to ride the horses home?"

"Why don't you go ahead, sir?" Erik answered quickly. "We'll manage fine."

Papa looked relieved. "I'd rather not leave Grandpa alone with the milking."

Erik lowered one eyelid in a long slow wink to Anders.

"I'll watch out for your little sister," he said. Taking care of Kate had become a joke between them.

But Kate didn't think it was funny. "I'll watch out for myself!" As Papa and Anders left, Kate turned her back on Erik and moved closer to watch Stretch.

"Your mare has small feet," he told Kate. "See the size of her shoes?" He compared them with a shoe he would put on Breeza.

When Stretch finished working, Kate and Erik swung up on the two horses. With a quick wave of the hand they left Stretch behind.

As Kate rode along, a breeze blew across an open field, catching the hair around her face. After the warmth of the day, the coolness felt good.

Soon they passed a farm where stumps dotted the land. Though Kate had ridden only her brother's horse before, she found it easy to handle the mare. When Kate moved the reins even slightly, Windsong responded to her request.

Erik leaned forward and stroked Breeza's neck. "You bought some good horses, Kate."

"I hope so." In the blacksmith shop she had started to wonder. If Papa had seen them act up, they would have gone back to Charlie.

"They're calm and steady," Erik said.

"But not when that man came to the shop." Kate felt concerned about that.

Erik grinned. "They sure didn't like him. Yet they've had good training somewhere."

"I just wish they were more spirited," Kate said. "Spirited in a good way, I mean."

Erik leaned back in the saddle. "You know how people act when they've been beaten down? Horses are the same way. When they're treated right, they show it."

"I keep thinking about the last owner," Kate said. "If a man is that awful to horses, what else would he do? Who else might he hurt?"

"What do you mean?" Erik asked.

"I wonder where that owner is now? There's a mystery with these horses, Erik. I want to know more. But I'm almost afraid to find out."

As Kate urged Windsong ahead, Breeza picked up his pace. Kate was slightly ahead of Erik when she saw a tree drop across the road.

Kate reined in. "What would make a tree fall down?" she asked, feeling uneasy. The midsized maple had a wide spread of leafy branches.

"Maybe someone's clearing his land," Erik answered. "We can still go around the tree."

On the left, a narrow opening lay between the top of the tree and the bushes at the edge of the road. When Erik started forward, Kate's mare edged ahead. But then as Windsong drew close to the tree, she stopped.

"Go on, girl," Kate said as the mare tossed her head. "There's room for you. Go around."

With Kate's encouragement, Windsong took one step, then another. The passageway was narrow, and the leaves of the tree thick. When Kate drew close to the branches, one of them trembled.

Startled, Windsong jerked, but she obeyed the pressure from Kate's legs. As the mare passed the branches, a man's hand reached out and grabbed her bridle.

Kate's heart leaped into her throat. Filled with terror, she gazed down, trying to see who held the bridle. A large hat hid his face.

"Giddyup!" Kate cried, urging the horse forward. But the man clung to Windsong's bridle, holding her back.

4

Papa's Warning

*A*n instant later Kate sensed Erik behind her. Reaching out, he slapped Windsong's rump. The mare lunged ahead, yanking the bridle from the man's hands. When he stumbled and fell back, Windsong bolted.

As though chased by a pack of dogs, Windsong lit off down the road. Clutching the reins, Kate leaned into the mare's neck.

She wanted only one thing—to be away from that awful man. But then Kate saw the blur of trees along the road. As though her life flashed before her, she knew what would happen if she landed beneath the flying hooves.

Stiff with fear, Kate grabbed Windsong's mane. As the galloping pace pounded against her body, Kate's panic grew. If she fell, it would be certain death.

"Slow her down!" Erik shouted.

"Whoa!" Kate cried. "Whoa!" In her panic Kate had almost forgotten what to do. But fear held the horse as certainly as it held Kate.

"Whoa!" she cried again. Tugging on the reins, she tightened the bit.

As Breeza moved alongside, Windsong dropped into a canter. "Keep her steady," Erik yelled to Kate, and she felt better just hearing him.

"It's all right, Windsong. It's all right," she kept repeating to the mare.

When Windsong responded to her voice, Kate patted her neck. "Good girl! You knew I needed to get away, didn't you?"

By the time Windsong slowed to a walk, they had gone some distance. It was only when they reined in that Kate started to tremble. Erik stopped beside her.

"What was that all about?" she asked. Though she tried to act calm, she couldn't stop shaking.

Erik looked grim. "When I told your dad I'd take care of you, I didn't expect an ambush!"

Nervously Kate giggled.

"It's not funny!" Erik looked angry and worried at the same time. "I don't know what that man was trying to do. Steal your horse or what!"

Taking a deep breath, Kate tried to push away her fear. "Maybe he knows about my silver dollars. Maybe he thinks I'm rich."

Erik scowled. "Stop making a joke of it! If I hadn't been right there, you would have been in big trouble."

Kate had no doubt that Erik was right. Deep down, she knew how serious the danger had been. Even so, she didn't want to admit how scared she felt.

"I've never heard of someone attempting a robbery like that," Erik said. "This has always been a safe place to live."

Turning around, he looked back. "Whoever that man is, he sure can't be trusted!"

Kate's hands tightened on the reins. As Windsong lifted her head, Kate leaned forward, talking to her.

"Did you see what the man looked like?" Erik asked.

Kate shook her head. "When his hand reached up, I was so scared I didn't think of much else."

"Neither did I. He wore a big hat—"

"A hat that hid his face." Even Kate's voice trembled. She rested her hands against her knees, trying to stop their shaking.

Erik noticed anyway. "I'm sorry," he said, and Kate knew he meant it. "I don't want to scare you even more, but we have to be careful. That man could follow us home. Then he'd know where you live."

Kate shivered. She had already thought of the same thing. She, too, looked around. "What should we do? We could hide in the trees and see if he comes past."

"Or we could try to stay ahead of him," Erik answered.

"Let's do that," Kate said. "We must have a good start."

Erik agreed. "I'm not anxious to meet him again with only the two of us."

Once more they urged the horses on. For a time they kept up a good pace with both Kate and Erik often looking back. When they reached a winding stretch of road they stopped the horses every once in a while to listen. Twice they wondered if they heard hoofbeats. Both times they decided they didn't.

When they finally came to the long, curving trail into Windy Hill Farm, they slowed the horses to a walk. Above the trees, the sun shone as if nothing could possibly be wrong. By the time they rode into the farm, Kate felt that Windsong truly belonged to her. In a strange way, the danger they had shared gave Kate respect for the mare.

Eager to have everyone admire Windsong, Kate directed her to the kitchen door. Erik followed with Breeza.

Kate's nine-year-old stepbrother, Lars, saw them coming. When he called back into the house, Kate's stepsister, Tina, hurried outside, followed by Mama.

The summer sun had multiplied Lars's freckles. "You bought two for the price of one?" he asked, sounding impressed.

Kate nodded. "But this is the horse I'll ride." As her hand came down on Windsong's mane, Kate felt a snarled mess.

Quickly she moved her hand, hoping the others wouldn't notice.

Mama walked all around Windsong and finally said, "She's a nice horse, and she's black like you wanted. Does she have some hair left over from winter?"

"The last owner didn't take care of her," Kate explained. "She needs good food and brushing down. We'll have both horses looking better in no time."

"Did Papa think it was a good buy?" Mama sounded as if she wanted to be positive, but wasn't sure what more to say.

"He knows I want to help the horses." Kate was becoming a bit uncomfortable.

"If Papa let you buy them, it'll be all right," Mama answered, as though trying to encourage her. "Papa hasn't been fooled yet. He knows horses."

"I hope so," Tina chimed in. She was speaking more English now than when Kate first met her.

Tina walked close, staring at Windsong's stomach. "Is your horse hungry?"

Lars shushed her. "Kate can't help that Windsong's ribs show."

"Papa said I can give her some extra oats," Kate said quickly.

"See, Tina?" Lars asked. "That's all Windsong needs."

"It has to be a good horse," Tina answered, her blue eyes wide. "It brought Kate all the way home."

"Thanks a lot!" As Kate turned Windsong, she caught Erik's grin.

By now Kate felt like a hot-air balloon with no air. The pride she had felt a short time ago had vanished. She tried to tell herself everything would be all right. But then she remembered the horses acting up in the blacksmith shop. *What if Windsong rears up when I'm riding her?*

Near the stable Kate slipped down from the horse. As she took the saddle from Windsong, Lars watched her every move.

Reaching up, he petted the mare. "I wish I had a horse like yours."

Just then Grandpa came out of the barn. He still limped from his fall on the ship coming to America. Seeing him, Kate grabbed Windsong's bridle and headed for a different door. If there was anything she didn't need it was someone else telling her how terrible the horse looked.

But Grandpa stepped in front of her, and Kate had to stop. Walking around Windsong, he studied her from every angle. After doing the same with Breeza, he spoke quickly in Swedish.

"They are good horses," Erik said, translating for Kate.

A heavy weight seemed to fall from Kate's shoulders. If Grandpa thought the horses were good, they would be.

When Erik left for home, Kate hurried into the small, one-room building the family used as a summer kitchen. Each spring Papa and Anders moved the wood cookstove here so it wouldn't heat up the main house.

Tonight the summer kitchen was still warm with the heat of the day, as well as the cooking. Yet the wonderful smells of supper reached out to Kate.

Feeling hollow with hunger, she sat down at the table. Her uncle Ben was gone tonight, as he usually was since getting a job at Nevers Dam. Even when Ben came home, he spent most of his time with Miss Sundquist, Kate's teacher at Spirit Lake School. But the rest of the family, along with Grandpa and Grandma, were there.

Since their arrival from Sweden, Mama's father and mother had lived with them. With her white hair waving back from her face, Grandma sat as straight as a young woman. Now she smiled as if telling Kate, "I'm proud to have you for my granddaughter."

While Grandma ate, she held baby Bernie in her arms. Already Kate's little brother was almost five months old. When he started to fuss, Kate jumped up to take him. Standing off to one side, she rocked back and forth. Bernie stared up at her, his eyes seeming to search her face.

With one finger Kate stroked his cheek. When he turned his mouth toward her hand, she laughed. "You aren't hungry! You were just fed!" She lifted him onto her shoulder and kept walking, rocking the baby as she went.

When Papa finished eating, he pushed back his plate. His face was as serious as Kate had ever seen him.

As he told Mama and the others about the fire at Charlie's stable, he said, "It's a warning about how fast something can happen. But for us there's a difference. We don't have a fire department just around the corner."

Across the table, Papa's gaze met Mama's. Then he looked from one person to the next.

"All of you have seen the dry fields and woods. They make me think of the great Hinckley fire."

Kate's nervous fingers twisted the cloth of her skirt. Everyone knew about that frightful fire. Thirteen years before, it had swept through four hundred square miles of Minnesota forests.

"It was close to this time of year," Papa went on. "September 1, 1894. The way things are, if a fire started here, it could burn the same way."

Tina sat with her blue eyes wide. Mama never allowed her to touch a match. Even the five-year-old knew the danger of one tiny flame.

"When you light a candle or lantern, don't let even one spark get away from you," Papa warned. Again he looked around the circle, making sure that everyone understood.

"I'll be careful," Anders promised.

"And you, Lars?"

"Yes, sir."

"Tina?" Papa asked. "No matches."

"Yes, Papa," the little girl answered.

As her stepfather's gaze met hers, Kate's heart thumped with the seriousness of what he asked.

"I promise, Papa," she told him. "You can trust me."

Papa nodded. Relaxing, he picked up his cup of coffee.

As Bernie shifted in Kate's arms, she glanced toward the

door. "Someone's here," she said quickly. In that instant she remembered the man on the road. Had he found them after all?

Clutching Bernie to her, Kate fought against fear.

5

Just Wait!

$\mathscr{A}$s the screen door swung open, it squeaked. Then Kate's six-foot, three-inch uncle stepped through. When Ben's gaze met Kate's, he grinned.

In spite of her fright, Kate's heart instantly softened.

Miss Sundquist, Kate's schoolteacher, was only a few steps behind. Standing next to Ben, Miss Sundquist seemed even smaller. As she said good evening to Grandpa and Grandma, her blue eyes sparkled.

"Have you eaten?" Mama asked quickly. Ben was her youngest brother.

When he shook his head, everyone shifted their chairs, making room at the table.

After stealing money in Sweden, Ben had run away to America. To set things right, he had sent money to the shop-keeper. Yet Ben's past sometimes came back to trouble him. More than once Kate had longed for a happier life for her uncle.

During the summer Miss Sundquist had often tutored Ben, teaching him to read and write English. Lately Kate had noticed that the books were put away early to give them time for a walk.

Tonight there seemed to be something special—almost a secret between them. *Ben has good news!* Kate thought.

Once Miss Sundquist reached out, and Ben took her hand, holding it beneath the table. Another time he gave her a long, slow smile. Kate felt sure she knew the reason.

At last the moment came. When Kate cleared away their dishes, Ben asked her to sit down.

"Jenny and I want to tell you something," he said.

Jenny, Kate thought with a start. She had never heard the teacher's first name before.

Again Ben took Miss Sundquist's hand. This time he didn't hide it beneath the table. "Jenny has given me the honor of promising to be my wife!"

"Oh, good!" Mama exclaimed. Her warm smile seemed to surround the couple.

"Yay!" Lars cheered. Tina clapped her hands while Anders had a wide grin.

"Congratulations!" Papa leaped to his feet, reaching out to shake both of their hands.

Grandpa's eyes filled with pride, but it was Grandma who said, "To think we came to America to see this!"

"When are you going to get married?" Mama asked the couple.

"As soon as I build a house on my land—*our* land," Ben answered.

"Your land?" This was a surprise to Grandpa.

"Yah, sure," Ben answered. "That is why I went to work at Nevers Dam. The wages are good, and my boss, Mr. Frawley, just gave me an even better job."

"A promotion?" Papa wanted to know.

Ben nodded. "Part of the time I'll still be night watchman. The rest of the time I'll work in the office."

"Doing books?" Papa asked.

Again Ben nodded. He had always been good at numbers. Even on his first day at Spirit Lake School he had solved every problem that Miss Sundquist had given him.

"Mr. Frawley is training me," Ben went on. "Both Jenny and I have saved money. We have put our dollars down on some land."

Ben glanced toward Papa. The look that passed between them told Kate that Papa had been in on this part of the secret.

Filled with curiosity, Kate leaned forward. "Where is your land, Ben?"

"Far, far away," he answered seriously. "So far you won't ever have to see us."

"Oh—" Tina sighed. Her blue eyes filled with tears. "I *want* to see you!"

Immediately Ben grinned. "You will, Tina. If you come with me, we will walk to the land."

"All of us?" Mama asked. "It's close enough to walk?"

"Well—" Ben thought about it. "Some of you might want to ride in the wagon. If we go right away, you can see the land before dark."

It took only a minute for all of them to pile out of the summer kitchen. In the barn the men worked quickly, harnessing Dolly and Florie, the Nordstroms' large draft horses. Carrying Windsong's bridle, Kate hurried outside. The mare was nibbling grass on the far side of the pasture.

Seeing her there, Kate remembered the whistle she had learned from Anders. Placing a thumb and finger between her lips, she blew hard. Windsong lifted her head and looked toward the barn.

Mama stared at Kate. "That wasn't very ladylike!"

Kate's cheeks burned with embarrassment. Ever since Anders taught her how, she had been careful not to whistle in front of Mama.

When Windsong returned to eating, Kate whistled again. The sound pierced the air, loud and long. "Hey, Windsong!" Kate shouted.

Again the mare lifted her head, this time as though remembering something from long ago. Moving slowly, she picked up one foot, then another. When Kate called a third time, the mare broke into a trot.

Grandma's smile for Kate was full of pride. As Windsong drew close, Kate held out a carrot.

"What a great horse you are!" she exclaimed. The carrot crunched between the mare's teeth.

When the farm wagon was ready, Papa jumped up to drive. Mama rode beside him with little Bernie. Grandpa and Grandma sat on the soft straw in the back.

"Where are you taking us?" Tina asked Ben as everyone set out. She slipped her small hand inside his big one, but Ben gave her no clue.

With Ben and Miss Sundquist walking ahead, they took the trail that passed through the farm. Before long, Ben led them onto a path branching off to the right.

In fifteen minutes they came to the banks of a creek. With the drought of summer the water ran low, yet the creek wound this way and that beneath tall pines.

"What a special place!" Kate exclaimed as Ben brought them to the knoll where he had started building his house. Already he had cut down pine trees, trimmed off the branches, and stripped the bark. Logs lay in place, two or three high, showing the outline of the house. More hewn logs lay on the ground, waiting to be notched and fit.

"How did you ever get all this work done?" Mama asked.

Ben grinned at Papa. "Carl helped me. We thought we'd surprise all of you."

Kate turned to Miss Sundquist. Kate still felt shy with this pretty young woman. But now, seeing the beginning of their house, the wedding seemed real. Just thinking about it filled Kate with excitement.

"You'll live right next to us! And you'll be my aunt!"

When Miss Sundquist smiled, Kate wanted to throw her arms around her. Just in time Kate thought better of it. Even though she was engaged to Ben, Miss Sundquist would be her teacher when school started again.

•

As though understanding how Kate felt, Miss Sundquist looked up at Ben. When she turned back to Kate, the teacher's smile lit her eyes. "There's something special we want to ask you," she said. "You're the one who got us together. Will you be my bridesmaid?"

"Me?" Overcome by surprise, Kate giggled. "You want *me* to be your bridesmaid?"

The teacher nodded. "We want *you!*"

"Really?" Kate asked. "Do you *really* think I can do it?"

"You betcha," Anders said quickly. "You'd make a good bridesmaid."

Kate stared at her brother. Such praise was rare, but she knew that he meant it.

Suddenly all the fun of being in a wedding welled up inside Kate. Again she wanted to throw her arms around her teacher. This time she asked. "Can I hug you, Miss Sundquist?"

The teacher laughed. "Only if you call me Jenny." It was Jenny who hugged Kate.

When they returned to Windy Hill Farm, Ben and Kate stopped at the fenced-in area next to the barn.

"There's something strange about your horses," he said.

"There are a lot of strange things about my horses!" Kate answered.

"You bought them from Charlie Saunders?" Ben's English was already surprisingly good. "I think I know where he got them."

"Charlie said it was a man from Nevers Dam. Do you know him?"

"Well, sort of." A shadow passed over Ben's face. "A few weeks ago I caught him stealing from the office."

Ben ran his fingers through his light brown hair. "I didn't want to say anything. When I've been a thief myself, it's hard to tell on someone else."

Kate saw the pain in her uncle's face. "You didn't have any choice."

Ben nodded. "I told him to put back the money. He

wouldn't do it. I had to tell my boss. Mr. Frawley fired the man."

"What was the man's name?" Kate asked quickly.

"He calls himself Dugan."

Kate didn't know anyone by that name. Yet strange things had been happening. "What does Dugan look like?" she asked.

"He's young," Ben said. "A swell—what do you call it?"

"A swell dresser."

"Yah. Sometimes he wore a tie, even to work."

"A tie!" Kate's mind leaped back to the blacksmith shop. She explained what had happened. "Would Dugan ever hang around Grantsburg?"

"I don't know why not," Ben answered. "Without a job he hasn't much to do."

"Did the horses like him?" Kate asked.

"They hated him," Ben told her. "Dugan was mean. I saw him beat them with a whip."

Ben walked into the stall and stroked Windsong's back. "See what a good horse she is? She just needs to be treated right."

Kate agreed. She was glad to know her uncle felt the same way.

"And the man, Dugan?" she asked. "What happened to him?"

Ben faced Kate. "I don't want to tell you."

"I think you better." Kate tried to sound calm, but her stomach churned. "I think I'll need to know."

Ben came out of the stall. "After the boss fired him, Dugan found me. He showed me his fist—"

Ben held up his own clenched fist. "He said, 'Just wait! I'll get even with you!'"

6

The Empty Barn

$\mathcal{K}$ate shivered. She couldn't help but feel afraid of this man Dugan. If he said such a thing to Ben, what else would he do?

"Is there any reason why Dugan would want to get even with me?" Kate asked, thinking about the stranger who tried to stop them on the way home.

"If Dugan knows that we're related—" Ben paused, as though not wanting to frighten her.

But Kate already felt scared in every part of her being. "Does Dugan know that you live here when you're not working?" she asked.

Ben thought about it. "Maybe. He worked in the office. He could have seen the list of workers and where we come from. Or maybe I told him without thinking about it. If Dugan knows you're my niece—" Ben's eyes darkened, as though dreading even the thought of Dugan making the connection.

"But there's something I did," Kate answered. "If it was Dugan at the blacksmith shop, I told him where I live. I also told him he hadn't taken care of his horses."

"You did?" Ben shook his head. "That's not so good."

Kate was starting to think the same thing. What had seemed an innocent conversation had already caused her all kinds of trouble.

"There's something I don't understand," she said. "Breeza and Windsong are good horses. Why didn't Dugan take care of them?"

"He is just not smart," Ben told her. "He doesn't take care of anything except himself."

Just then Lars called them. As they walked toward the house, Ben stopped halfway. "Kate, you have to be careful," he warned. "Dugan doesn't think like other people. He's so full of anger that—"

"That what?" Kate asked.

"Dugan hates me so much he might try to get even through you," Ben answered. "He could do anything—even something crazy."

When they joined the rest of the family, Ben's worry seemed to fall off like an old coat. Each time he looked at Jenny, he appeared to be a carefree, happy young man. Only Kate had seen what was really inside.

"I baked a cake today," Mama told him. "Let's use it to celebrate your engagement."

When Ben left to take Jenny home, Kate lit a farm lantern and went outside. She wanted to say good-night to her new horses without anyone else there.

Near the summer kitchen Kate looked around. Neither of her brothers was in sight. Without making a sound, Kate reached the barn and slipped inside.

Walking quickly, she passed through to the fenced-in area on the other side. Breeza was drinking from the large water tank. At the gate leading to the road, Windsong stood nosing the latch.

Moving slowly so she wouldn't frighten the mare, Kate walked over. Windsong lifted her head as though she recognized Kate. Reaching up, she stroked Windsong's shoulder.

"How do you like your new home?" Kate snapped a lead rope to Windsong's halter and led the mare to the barn.

As she drew close to the door, Kate glanced around. Breeza was just behind. When Kate stopped, Breeza stopped, as though waiting to see where Kate took the mare.

The horse stalls were at the west end of the barn. High board walls separated the horses one from another. Dolly and Florie were already munching oats. Next to them was Wildfire, the mare that belonged to Anders.

On the other side of Wildfire were three empty stalls. Kate led Windsong into the middle one of the three. Without Kate saying a word, Breeza walked into the stall on Windsong's left.

Looping the lead rope for an easy release, Kate tied it into the ring in Windsong's stall. When Kate returned with another rope, Breeza stood waiting, as though to say, "I'm here. Get me ready for a good night's sleep."

His expression struck Kate funny. "You keep each other good company!" She felt glad that she had bought both of them.

When Kate went back to the mare, Windsong was chewing on the end of her lead rope.

"C'mon, girl, you aren't that hungry," Kate told her. At the oat bin she took a portion for both horses. Then she found a scissors and brush and comb.

When Kate started working on Windsong's mane, she found it so tangled that the job seemed impossible. The mare stood still, as though she knew Kate was trying to help her. Even so, Kate finally gave up and started brushing the mare's shaggy coat.

As long black hairs fell out, Kate kept brushing. With every passing moment, she felt more angry at the man who had let the horse get this way. Then she remembered Ben's words. *"Just wait!"* Dugan had said. *"I'll get even with you!"*

Kate had no doubt that Dugan would do what he said.

But *how* was the question. How would Dugan try to get even?

As though Ben were still speaking, Kate heard his warning. *"Dugan hates me so much, he might try to get even through you."* Kate felt scared just thinking about what that might mean.

Windsong's bony ribs stuck out as if she hadn't eaten well for months. If Dugan could do that to a horse, what might he do to a person he hated?

"You need a lot of oats," Kate told the mare.

As though liking the sound of Kate's voice, Windsong looked up from eating. When dust and old hair fell away, the mare switched her tail, as if feeling better about herself.

It made Kate curious. Could a horse feel pride in herself? Kate didn't know. Yet now and then Windsong almost seemed human.

Pulling Windsong's hair from the brush, Kate turned toward the lantern. The small flame didn't give nearly as much light as she would like. Just then Kate heard a strange thud.

What is it? she wondered, instantly alert.

The noise had come from outside—from close by, it seemed. Had someone tripped, then caught himself against the wall? As Kate whirled around, a shadow slid across the window.

For a moment Kate waited, watching. The shadow had moved quickly—so quickly that Kate wasn't sure what she had seen. Could it be a cloud moving across the moon?

Just the same, Kate hurried over to the barn door. Through the open upper half she looked out. Shadows darkened the side wall of the barn. As far as she could tell, no one was there.

I imagined it, Kate decided as she returned to the mare. Once more she looked at the tangled mane. How could *anyone* let a horse get this way?

Pushing her scared feelings aside, Kate went back to work on Windsong's mane. As she reached up, the brush flipped out of her hand, fell against Windsong, and dropped to the ground. Suddenly Windsong bent her forelegs beneath her. Dropping down on her knees, she touched the dirt with her muzzle.

Kate stared at her. "If I didn't know that horses don't bow, I'd think that's what you're doing!"

Looking up, Windsong moved her lips.

Kate giggled. For all the world, the horse seemed to be trying to talk. Kate wished that she could—that somehow Windsong would tell her all that she knew. But then the mare got up, once more standing as any horse would.

In that instant Kate heard a creak in the floorboards directly overhead. Someone was in the loft!

Kate froze, listening. As she strained to catch any sound, she thought of the shadow. Maybe she had seen someone after all. Had that person come in a door at the other end of the barn?

Then Kate had an even scarier thought. *Could there be two people? One outside? One in here?*

Three ladders led upward into the loft. Two were at the far end of the barn, away from Kate. Closer to the horses was a third opening. Yet that hole was also outside the circle of light from the lantern. Deep shadows lay along the wall.

Just then Kate heard another creak in the floorboards. No doubt about it—someone was in the hayloft!

Earlier that summer Papa had filled the loft with first-crop hay. Even a big person could walk there without making much noise.

As footsteps crossed the floor to the opening and the ladder, Kate remembered the man on the road. *Maybe he followed us home! Maybe it's Dugan!*

Seconds later Kate heard someone on the ladder. Darkness hid whoever it was.

Kate spun around. Filled with panic, she searched for a way of escape. But the ladder lay between her and the nearest door.

Already it was too late. *What if he finds me alone?*

7

The Disappearing Horse

*N*ear where the lantern hung, Kate spied a pitchfork and snatched it up. Holding the fork in front of her, she faced whoever hid in the darkness.

On the dirt floor of the barn she could barely hear his footsteps. *Sneaky as a cat!* Kate thought.

Just then he stepped into the ring of light.

"Lars!" Feeling foolish about her fear, Kate lowered the pitchfork. "What are you doing here?"

Her younger brother shrugged. "Just looking around."

"Just looking!" Kate's fright turned to anger. "Hasn't anyone ever told you not to sneak up on someone?"

"I wasn't sneaking." Lars sounded resentful. "I was just curious."

"Curious, my eye! If I hadn't heard you, you would have scared me to death." Kate eyed him suspiciously. "How long have you been in the barn?"

Lars shrugged. "Half an hour maybe. When I heard you coming, I snuck up in the loft."

"You've been here half an hour?" Once more Kate felt afraid. "You're sure?"

Lars thought about it. "Maybe forty-five minutes."

That's even worse! Kate pushed the thought aside, trying to tell herself that she had imagined the shadow. Yet she hadn't imagined the thud against the wall. If someone was there, it couldn't have been Lars.

"Why are you here?" she asked him again.

In the light of the lantern Lars raised his chin. "I wanted to see the horses."

"Why?" Kate wanted to know. "Are you planning to ride one of them?"

Lars stared at her. "You have two horses, and you aren't going to let me ride *one*? You let Erik ride Breeza. Why can't I?"

"Because—" Kate started to tell him how the horses had acted up in Grantsburg. Then she remembered how honest Lars was. If he told Papa, the horses would go back to Charlie's stable.

"You can't ride them because I don't want you to," Kate said.

"Fine sister you are!" Lars exclaimed. "How selfish can you be?"

"I don't want you to get hurt," Kate said lamely. Even to her own ears, the excuse sounded weak.

Lars hooted. "I rode horses long before you came to this farm! I'm nine years old, but I'm taller than you!"

Kate straightened to her full height. "I own the horses, and you have to ask my permission first."

Lars flushed. Turning, he looked at Windsong, as though to hide his hurt. "You sure have a homely horse!"

"What do you know about it?" But Kate felt terrible inside.

"She looks like she hasn't been brushed in a coon's age."

"I just spent at least an hour brushing her," Kate said stiffly.

"Do you want me to show you how?"

"I know how," Kate answered. "I just have to do it a lot of times. She'll start looking better."

"All right!" Lars sounded as if it didn't matter to him. But his eyes had the look of a wounded animal.

He feels left out, Kate thought as her brother hurried toward the door. Always she and Anders and Erik did things together. How often had they included Lars?

Not liking the answer to her own question, Kate started after him. She didn't like hurting her younger brother.

Then Kate stopped. What if Lars told Papa? Kate didn't want to lose the horses. Not for anything.

But Lars turned back. "I think you have a circus horse."

Kate stared at him. "You do? Why do you think that?"

"Why should I tell *you*?"

Kate shrugged. "You don't have to. But let's make a trade. If you promise to keep a secret, I'll tell you why I don't want you to ride the horses. And you can tell me why you think Windsong is a circus horse."

"Wel-l-l-l—" Lars wasn't sure. "What's the secret?"

"Promise you won't tell?"

"Tell what? I don't know what I'm promising."

Kate waited until curiosity got the better of Lars.

"All right," he said. "I promise."

As Kate told Lars how the horses acted in Grantsburg, she watched her brother's eyes. "Don't forget you promised," she said as she finished. "You can't tell Papa."

"Why not?" Lars asked, just as honest as Kate expected. "Horses are different with different people. Didn't you say they didn't like that man at the blacksmith shop? Dugan, did you call him?"

Kate nodded. "That's who I think he is."

"If Dugan was mean to them, they'd remember," Lars said.

Kate stared at him. Maybe Lars was right. Yet she was afraid to find out by telling Papa.

"So why do you think Windsong's a circus horse?" Kate asked.

Lars looked up at the ceiling above Windsong's stall.

"See that knothole? I was watching you. I saw Windsong bow."

"It *was* a bow, wasn't it?" Kate felt excited that Lars recognized it. "But why would that make her a circus horse?"

"Remember when we went to the circus?" Lars asked. "When you and Anders were busy, I watched a man who trains horses. He showed me some of their tricks."

Lars picked up the brush Kate had used and walked over to Windsong. Using the brush, Lars gently tapped the upper part of the mare's foreleg. Windsong bowed to the ground.

"See?" Lars grinned. "See what I told you? Now isn't that a trained horse for you?"

The sun had just edged over the horizon when Kate slipped from the house the next morning. With two carrots in her pocket she headed for the barn.

She was partway there when Lutfisk barked. A moment later he ran up to her.

"Good boy!" Kate dropped to her knees and scratched the dog behind his ears. "Where have you been?"

Named for the dried cod that Swedes eat at Christmas, Lutfisk belonged to Anders. Now he yipped, then ran away from Kate to dodge behind the corner of the granary.

"Hey, Lutfisk!" Kate called. Anders had taught the dog to play hide-and-seek, and he wanted Kate to follow him. When she didn't, he returned to her.

"All right, *Lute fisk*." As Kate drawled the dog's name, he wagged his tail with pleasure. "Where were you last night when I needed you?"

When Kate went into the barn, Lutfisk bounded along next to her, then ran ahead. Suddenly he stopped. Sitting down directly in front of Kate, he tipped his head to one side and barked.

Kate laughed. "I know. We have some new horses."

Once again Lutfisk bounded away. At the other end of

the barn, Papa, Anders, and Ben were already milking cows. When Lutfisk reached Windsong, he sniffed around the mare's heels.

Owning both horses still seemed unreal to Kate. She couldn't believe they were really hers. After talking to Windsong a bit, Kate moved closer, letting the mare get used to her again.

At the front of the stall the lead rope was loose. "What did I do wrong?" Kate asked herself, still talking aloud. "I must not have tied it right."

Telling herself not to do that again, Kate loosened the rope the rest of the way. She led Windsong and Breeza to the fenced-in area outside the barn, then let them into the pasture.

Like a child let out of school, Windsong raced across the field. Back and forth, from one end to the other she cantered, her long mane and tail flying in the wind. Breeza followed, and Lutfisk ran alongside, yipping as if he enjoyed his new friends.

Kate climbed up on the rail fence. Once Windsong drew close, as if to check her out. Then she leaped away, making large circles around the stumps in the field. On the far side of the pasture she stopped, put down her head, and nosed the grass.

After watching the horses for a while, Kate whistled for Windsong. This time she came right away. When the mare drew close, Kate held out a carrot. "C'mon, Windsong! C'mon! Good for you!"

Close behind Windsong, Breeza followed like a shadow. The second carrot went to him. Kate petted both horses, feeling pleased about the way they had come to her.

Catching Windsong's halter, Kate snapped on a lead rope and took her into the barn. After tying the rope to the ring at the front of the stall, Kate returned for Breeza.

When Kate led him into the barn, she found Windsong backing out of her stall. Kate stared at her. "I'm sure I tied your rope!" This time she was careful to get the rope exactly the way Anders taught her.

After giving each of them a measure of oats, Kate started grooming Breeza. She had set her mind on getting both horses satiny smooth. She was only partway through brushing them when Mama called her for breakfast.

As Kate stepped inside the summer kitchen, she found her brothers' blankets and pillows were already picked up. When Grandpa and Grandma came from Sweden, Mama and Papa had given them their room on the main floor of the house. While Mama and Papa used the upstairs bedroom, Anders and Lars slept in the small, one-room summer kitchen. If Ben came home, he, too, rolled out a blanket on the floor.

Now the family was gathered around the table.

"I'll help you shock oats today," Ben told Papa as Kate sat down.

But Papa shook his head. "You don't have many days off from the dam. You need to work on your house."

"You're sure?" Even as he asked, Ben looked relieved.

"I'm sure," Papa answered. "It won't take long on the oats."

He glanced toward Mama, and their gaze met and held. It seemed they were talking without words. Kate wondered what they were telling each other.

When everyone finished eating, Papa read to them from the Bible and prayed. Then he, Anders, and Grandpa left to work in the oat field south of the house. Lars went out to feed the pigs.

As soon as Kate could get away, she returned to the barn. Dolly, Florie, and Wildfire were gone, and Kate knew the men were using them to shock oats. Breeza turned his head to gaze at Kate, but Windsong's stall was empty.

That's strange! Kate thought. Papa wouldn't have taken her without asking permission. Besides, he would have hitched Windsong to Breeza, not to Wildfire.

"Where's your friend?" Kate asked Breeza. The more

Kate thought about it, the more puzzled she felt. Then she remembered Lars. "He's probably riding Windsong!"

Kate hurried from the barn. Outside, the gate to the pasture stood open. But where was Windsong?

"Lars is going to catch it for this!" she muttered.

8

Where There's Smoke . . .

*A*nger welled up inside Kate. She slipped through the gate, slammed it shut, and latched it. Shielding her eyes against the sun, she gazed across the pasture.

At first she saw only cows. When she climbed up on the rails of the wood fence, she got a better look. There, next to the woods, Kate saw something larger. Something black. Windsong!

Kate breathed a sigh of relief. But then, like a freshly kindled fire, her anger grew. *Lars must have let her out. No one else was here to do it!*

One moment Kate felt scared about what could have happened to her brother. *What if Windsong acted up? What if Lars had been hurt, even killed?*

The next moment Kate felt angry that she had trusted Lars with a secret. *Stupid brother! He took advantage of me!*

Kate flipped her braid over her shoulder. She would get this settled with Lars right now.

As Kate hurried back to the summer kitchen, Mama came outside.

"Have you seen Lars?" Kate asked.

"He's with Papa, isn't he?" her mother answered. "Is something wrong?"

"I hope not!" Kate did not explain.

"Will you take morning coffee to Papa?" Mama asked.

From the summer kitchen she brought a basket filled with cookies, sandwiches, and a gallon jar of homemade root beer. Another jar held coffee for Papa and Grandpa.

Papa and the others were shocking oats at the far end of the field in front of the house. As Kate drew closer to them, she saw Grandpa riding on the binder. The large reel laid the oats with the heads of grain all in one direction. From there they passed to the part of the machine that tied them in bundles.

Anders and Papa followed behind, setting the bundled stalks upright. With about ten bundles leaning against each other, the heads of grain could dry.

The minute Anders saw Kate, he stopped working. Pulling off his straw hat, he wiped his forehead with a red bandana. "Just in time!"

As Kate set the basket on the freshly cut field, her anger spilled out. "Where's Lars?"

Papa glanced toward the edge of the field. "He went to the spring for milk."

Lars was just coming over the edge of the hill. Unwilling to talk in front of the others, Kate ran toward him.

"What do you mean by letting Windsong out?" she demanded.

Lars stared at her. "*I* let Windsong out? What are you talking about?"

"Who else would do it?" Kate asked. "Everyone else is working!"

"Is that so?" Lars exclaimed. "I'm working too!"

In his hand Lars held a bucket of milk. In his eyes there was resentment. "I didn't take your dumb horse, if that's what you're wondering."

Kate glared at him. "It's not what I'm wondering. It's

what I'm thinking. If you didn't take Windsong, how did she get out in the pasture?"

Lars shrugged. "I don't know, and I don't care."

Kate's anger rushed to the surface again. "You don't *care*?"

"Why should I care?" Lars's voice rose in anger. "You have two horses, and you won't let me touch either one! Last night I got the worst end of the bargain!"

Scared that Lars would say more, Kate glanced over her shoulder. Papa, Anders, and Grandpa were all listening. Kate felt sure they had heard.

Ready to defend herself, Kate opened her mouth. Instead, she saw Grandpa's expression. Though he didn't understand all the English words, Grandpa knew exactly what was happening.

Seeing his kind old eyes, Kate felt embarrassed. Grandpa had respected her. Now he was seeing another side. Like Erik, Grandpa was no doubt disappointed.

A hot flush burned Kate's cheeks. *And I wanted Erik to admire me! I wanted to make my family proud!*

Unwilling to face Grandpa and the others, Kate started back across the field. The stubble left from the freshly cut oats crackled with dryness. Dragging her feet, Kate stared at the ground. With each step her misery grew.

When she reached the beehives at the edge of the field, Kate looked back. Papa and the others sat on the ground, eating. Around them, more than half of the field was already shocked. For the first time Kate realized there was something different from last year.

Through all her mixed-up emotions, Kate gazed at the shocks of grain, forcing herself to think. What was it?

Then Kate knew. More than once in the past month Papa had looked concerned. After living in the city most of her life, Kate hadn't understood what it meant. But here, near the edge of the field where a few stalks had been missed, she could see for herself. The shocks of oats were far apart because there weren't many stalks to put in them. The heads of grain were dry and small.

Not wanting to face the truth, Kate hurried toward the house. Yet she couldn't leave her awful thoughts behind. *There hasn't been enough rain for the crops to grow.*

————

When Anders came in for the noon meal, he found Kate grooming Windsong in the barn. "You know, Kate, maybe you were a bit hard on Lars."

Kate stared at Anders. This peacemaking role seemed out of character for her tall, teasing brother. "So you're sticking up for Lars now?" she asked.

"Nope! Just trying to save you from yourself!"

Kate glared at him.

"I mean it! I don't think Lars let Windsong out. Some horses know how to untie a lead rope. They pull it with their teeth."

In spite of her anger, Kate realized that his words made sense. Twice Kate had found Windsong's lead rope untied. Another time it was loose.

"But what about the pasture gate?" Kate asked. "How could Windsong open that?"

"With her nose," Anders said. "She just pushes up the latch. If Breeza had been loose, he would have followed Windsong."

Kate groaned. "What should I do?" she asked.

Anders led her out to the gate. With a piece of wire he showed Kate how to fix the latch so the mare couldn't open it. "You're just lucky Windsong didn't open the gate to the road."

As they started back to the barn, Anders leaned forward. "You know, I'm really concerned about you, Kate."

"About me?" she asked. "That's a surprise!" It seemed too good to be true.

"You betcha." Anders peered at her face. "Is that a pimple I see on your nose?"

Kate jerked back. Only that morning she had stood in front of the mirror, wondering what to do about the small red spot.

Anders shook his head. "It's like a bright pink rose turning to deep red."

In spite of being thirteen years old, Kate stuck out her tongue. But Anders had no mercy.

"If you have a pimple on your nose, Erik will never like you!" he warned.

Kate glared at him. "Anders Nordstrom! I hate the ground you walk on!"

"Maybe," he answered calmly. "But maybe there's something you need to learn from me."

"There's not a thing I could possibly learn from you!" Kate stalked off.

Anders called after her. "I'll show you another way to tie a rope. It's a way where no horse on earth can get loose."

Kate turned around. "But what if Windsong ever *needs* to get loose?"

"You have to be there to cut the rope," Anders said. And he meant it.

———

As Kate came out of the barn, she saw Papa working at their three beehives. Now in early August each of those hives looked like a tall white building.

Bees crawled in and out of the entrances. More bees filled the air, returning home with nectar. Careful to not step between their flight and the hive, Kate moved closer.

Seeing her, Papa grinned. "This hot, dry weather is good for something!" All summer the bees had stayed busy, collecting pollen and nectar.

The bottom part of each hive was made up of deep boxes called hive bodies. Each of those boxes was filled with frames on which the bees built honeycomb. In the small, hexagon-shaped holes, the queen laid her eggs and worker bees stored honey and pollen.

By now the hives were high with supers—shallower boxes that Papa added to the top. Supers also held frames on which the bees built honeycomb. From those frames Papa would take the honey that the bees didn't need for winter.

"If all goes well, we'll have a good supply of honey!" he told Kate.

"If all goes well?" she asked. "What could happen?"

"Ohhhh—" Papa sounded as if he didn't want to borrow trouble. "Skunks swat the side of the hives. When the bees come out, the skunks gather them up and eat them."

"Eat them?" Kate couldn't imagine eating a mouthful of bees.

"But the worst thing would be a bear," Papa said. "We don't see them often, but—"

"A bear?" Kate's stomach tightened. Before she moved to northwest Wisconsin, her friend Sarah had warned her about bears. Only lately had Kate started to believe that the woods were safe.

"They really tear open a hive." Papa lifted off a cover, looked inside, and added another super. "You know how bees glue the hive boxes together? It's work prying them apart. But a bear is so strong that nothing stops him."

Papa shook his head, as if he didn't want to think about it. "We'll harvest the honey soon."

Kate guessed what he was thinking. *So we get it out of harm's way.*

————

After supper, Papa and Grandpa, Anders and Lars walked over to Ben's house to help with the building. Mama went outside to check the rain barrels she used for washing clothes.

Though their well gave a good supply of water, it was full of iron and left orange streaks on the clothes. Instead of using that water for her washing, Mama took rainwater that came off the roof through the spouts into barrels at each corner of the house. But now that water was getting low.

Pumping bucket after bucket, Kate carried water to Mama's beans and tomato plants and the fruit trees planted years before.

Near the garden was what Kate had called "Mama's grass." Last summer Papa had started that grass between the house and the barn. Early in the summer Kate and the others had tried to keep it alive.

But then Mama stopped them. "You have to water our big garden," she said. "You can't do both."

"I can try," Kate told her. She knew the grass was part of Mama—part of wanting something beautiful at her door, instead of dirt.

But Mama shook her head. On the way back to the summer kitchen, she took one last look at the grass. Within just a few days it had turned as brown and dry as everything else.

"When it rains your grass will come back," Kate told her mother now. "It will be green again."

"Yah, sure," Mama answered. But she turned away, as if she didn't want to see the dead-looking grass.

When there was no longer enough daylight to work, Ben and the others returned from his house. Ben looked excited about all that he and the others had built. "Soon Jenny and I can get married!" he told Kate.

———————

Long before dawn, Kate heard Ben take his horse from the barn and ride off for Nevers Dam. Soon after the sun edged above the horizon, Kate slipped from the house into the cool morning. She found it a welcome relief to pull on a sweater.

At the barn Kate saddled Windsong. Riding the mare, she took the cutoff to Ben's house. A pressed-down line of grass marked a trail between the trees.

Before long, Windsong came out of the woods. As Kate looked ahead, Ben's house rose from the knoll near the creek. The ground sloped upward, well above where the creek flowed in spring flooding.

Now the early morning sun shone on the log walls. Ben and the others had worked hard. The house stood proudly, six or seven logs high. Soon Ben would put up the cross poles for the floor of the loft.

Reining in, Kate sat there for a moment, touched by the beauty of the place. Miss Sundquist had always been her favorite teacher. Kate could hardly wait to be her bridesmaid. Yet it was more than that. Kate wanted to see both Ben and Miss Sundquist happy.

Not Miss Sundquist, Kate corrected herself. *Jenny*. It seemed too good to be true that such a special person would soon be part of their family.

Like a pesky fly, the memory of Dugan's threat broke into the morning stillness. According to Ben, Dugan was full of hate. What might he do to get even? If only they knew, they could protect Ben and Jenny.

And me, Kate added to herself. *What could Dugan do to hurt me?*

As Windsong tossed her head, Kate tried to push away her fear. Instead, her muscles tightened with dread.

"God, please help them!" Kate's prayer spilled out. "Keep Ben safe. Keep Jenny safe. Help us know what to do."

Feeling peaceful again, Kate once more looked toward Ben's house. Suddenly she sniffed.

"It's my imagination!" Kate told herself, then realized she had spoken aloud.

"Do all you can to be careful," Papa had said more than once. *"Only one stray spark and everything will go up in smoke."*

Kate tried to push aside her worry. Papa had warned them so often that she was getting jumpy. Just the same, she sniffed again.

No longer could she fool herself. The wind was carrying the smell right to her.

In that moment Kate saw it. A thin wisp of smoke, barely visible against the blue sky. A wisp of smoke from inside Ben's house.

9

The Ugly Message

"Giddyup!" Kate touched her heels on the mare's sides.

Windsong surged forward, then broke into a gallop. With each step Kate could see the smoke better. There was a fire all right, and no one else was around.

In no time at all Windsong covered the remaining distance. When they reached the house, Kate slid down from the saddle and ran through the open door.

Inside, a heap of rubbish lay where the logs formed a corner. What looked like pine branches and old gunnysacks were pushed against the bottom logs. The wall had caught fire, and the smoke curled upward.

Kate headed for the creek. When she reached the water, she pulled off her sweater and dropped it in. With a quick movement she yanked it out and tore back to the house. There she swatted the sweater against the fire.

Again and again Kate pounded the rubbish and logs. Under the wet sweater, the flame slowed down, but the fire didn't go out. Kate felt sure it had smoldered for a time, eating into the logs.

Frantically she looked around. If only—

Was there a bucket anywhere?

Then Kate remembered. The last time she was here she had seen one. Ben had used it to carry water from the creek. Where was it now?

Leaving her wet sweater on the smoldering pine branches, Kate ran outside. When she found the bucket, she hurried to the creek. Kneeling down, she filled the bucket, then ran up the bank to the house. Aiming carefully, she threw the water against the burning wall.

By the time she had made several trips, Kate was out of breath and panting with exhaustion. Finally even the embers in the log walls were out. Only then did Kate dare to sit down. Only then did she realize the awfulness of what had happened.

The burned logs were at the bottom corner of two walls. Because the logs were notched together, Ben would have to tear the house apart, log by log, to take them out. If he didn't, he'd always have a weak wall.

"Oh, Ben!" Kate felt so bad that she spoke aloud. "It'll set you back so much!" Kate knew how much her uncle wanted to finish the house so he and Jenny could get married. Her uncle had put every spare moment into finishing it before winter.

Then Kate remembered the woods with its carpet of dry leaves. In no time at all, the fire could have raced through the trees all the way to Windy Hill Farm. With a strong wind the fire could have burned every other house in the area.

Kate trembled. Filled with the awfulness of it, she realized something even worse. The fire must have been set. There was no other explanation for what had happened. Who had done such a terrible thing?

Dugan said he was going to get even. Like a fist pounding a wall, Ben's words struck Kate's heart. *Who* is *this man who hates Ben so?*

Filled with panic, Kate knew something else. She, too, was in danger. Who was lurking around this lonely place?

If it was Dugan, was he still nearby? Had he even watched while she put out the fire?

Kate leaped to her feet. *I've got to tell Papa right away.* In that moment she remembered Windsong.

When Kate bounded outside, she saw the mare nearby. With her reins dragging in the water, she drank from the creek.

Kate tumbled down the bank. Reaching Windsong, she gathered the reins. Holding the mare's bridle, Kate led her up the steep bank.

When Windsong nuzzled her arm, Kate felt a strange comfort. In everything that happened, Windsong seemed to understand.

At the top of the knoll outside Ben's house, Kate put her arm around the mare's neck. "How do you know so much?" she asked. Reaching up, she stroked the horse between her eyes.

"It's good to have you along," Kate said, grateful for the mare's company. "You'll help me, won't you?"

As though answering, Windsong nodded her head.

Kate giggled. "What a friend you are! You even agree with me!"

With Kate in the saddle, Windsong headed for home. Soon they entered the woods. As the trees arched above them, Kate felt relieved. For this one day, at least, no fire had raced through their branches. But then, on a straight section of trail, the mare suddenly stopped.

"Go on, Windsong!" Kate flicked the reins.

Unwilling to move, the horse stood there.

"C'mon, girl! I have to get back. The fire might start up again!"

Windsong's ears turned toward Kate, listening. But when Kate clucked to her, the mare tossed her head.

Kate was getting upset. "You've always obeyed before. What's stopping you now?"

Kate tightened her legs, but Windsong refused to move.

As Kate urged her on, the mare planted her feet as if rooted there.

"Windsong!" Kate cried. "I have to get home. Whoever set that fire has to be caught!"

No matter what Kate said, Windsong would not budge. Finally Kate slipped down from the saddle. As she took the bridle, the mare tossed her head. Eyes wide, her nostrils flared.

Kate hung on. Walking in front of Windsong, Kate led her along the trail. More than once, the mare tugged at the bridle, as though trying to get away.

When the mare finally settled down, Kate swung up into the saddle. Strangely, Windsong obeyed her again. At Kate's urging, she broke into a trot, then a canter. Filled with the need to find Papa, Kate felt relieved.

As she rode up to the farmhouse, Mama crossed the yard.

"Kate! What happened?" she asked.

Only then did Kate realize how dirty she was. She had washed her hands in the creek, but her dress was covered with soot.

Before she could explain, Anders came out of the barn. "You look like you've been playing in the mud!"

When Anders walked closer, his grin disappeared. "It's soot! Where's the fire?"

Kate started to tell him, but Anders stopped her. "Just a minute," he said, and ran to get Papa.

Quickly Kate told all of them what had happened. Papa took one look at Anders.

"We better get over and check around."

At the pasture Papa and Anders caught Breeza and Wildfire. Riding bareback, they set off with Kate still on Windsong.

"Something else happened," Kate told Papa as they headed toward Ben's. "On the way home, Windsong wouldn't obey me. You know that straight stretch of trail partway through the woods? She stopped there and wouldn't go on."

"You did everything you usually do to get Windsong to obey?"

Kate nodded.

"Well, we can't have that," Papa answered. "If she thinks she can get by with something, she'll keep doing it."

When they reached the same spot, Windsong stopped again. Breeza and Wildfire also refused to go on.

"This is where you were before?" Papa asked Kate. "There could be a bear around."

"A *bear*?" Kate's heart thumped. She stared into the woods. The leaves hung heavy from the trees. Branches and bushes made it hard to see more than a short distance away. Was there a bear hiding somewhere behind those leaves? A bear ready to pounce on them?

"Our bears usually aren't dangerous," Papa told Kate. "But I wouldn't want to get between a female and her cubs."

When they reached Ben's house, Kate led Papa and Anders inside. The charred logs glistened in the morning sun. For a long moment Papa stood in front of them, staring into the corner that had burned. Finally he shook his head.

"You put this out by yourself, Kate?" he asked.

Kate nodded. As she looked at the burned logs, her fear returned. Even the charred smell bothered her.

"You were very brave," Papa said. "You caught the fire when it was still small. But I'm awfully glad you weren't hurt. If you ever see a fire out of control—"

"I know," Kate answered. "I shouldn't try to put it out by myself."

As though she were reliving the nightmare, she saw the smoke curl upward. "It had just started, and the creek was right here."

Even Anders seemed impressed. "Wow, Kate! I'm proud of you!"

Kate blinked with surprise. *He's changing*, she thought. For the second time in two days, Anders had offered rare encouragement. Kate felt the warmth of his approval.

"You must have worked like crazy to get enough water," Anders said.

"I did," Kate answered. Just thinking about all the trips up and down the bank, she felt out of breath. Again she remembered the terror of seeing the fire, of being the only one here to put it out.

"Kate," Papa said gently, and she knew the fear must have shown in her face.

When she couldn't speak, Papa went on. "I want to pray for you."

Standing inside the house with no roof, Papa took off his old straw hat. Bowing his head, he spoke quietly, as if certain that God was right there with them.

"I thank thee, Father," Papa prayed, and Kate squeezed her eyes shut. "I thank thee for protecting Kate. I ask thee to take away her fear. Show her how much you love her."

Startled, Kate raised her head. How did Papa know? How did he know that deep down she felt so afraid that she could barely breathe?

Then from the woods she heard a bird chirping. It chirped as though its nest had always been safe, as if nothing had happened that could have taken it away.

Strangely, Kate felt comforted. When she opened her eyes, she saw Anders with his head still bowed, praying.

"There will always be times when you're afraid," Papa told them. "But if you know deep down that God loves and protects you, you'll make it through."

Calmly, as if nothing important had happened, Papa went back to studying Ben's walls. "Even though you caught the fire, there's a lot of damage," he said. "He can't have weak logs at the bottom."

"Will Ben have to start over?" Kate asked.

"I think we should ask Big Gust to come out. He could lift that part of the wall and help us replace the burned logs. Otherwise Ben will have to take everything apart."

Papa put his straw hat back on his head. "You didn't see anyone around, did you, Kate?"

"Not at the house," she told him. "I didn't look in the woods."

"Good," Papa answered. "I'm glad you didn't."

"I didn't want to stay here by myself," Kate said. "Whoever started the fire had plenty of time to get away."

When they were ready to leave, Kate circled the house, walking a different way than when they came. In the packed-down dirt someone had carved out a message. Kate stared at the words.

I told you
I'd get even

"What a horrible thing to say!" Kate cried out.

In that instant her sense of God's love was stripped away. All the fear Kate had felt during the fire returned.

This wasn't a child playing games. This message was meant for Ben, and for anyone else who cared about him.

10

Big Discovery

"*K*ate!" Anders called from inside the house. "C'mon, we're going!"

But Kate stood there, unable to speak.

"Hurry up!" Anders shouted as he came around the corner. "Papa wants to go back."

In the next instant Anders looked into Kate's face. "What's wrong? You're white as a ghost!"

"It's Dugan!" Kate whispered.

Anders looked down. "Oh-oh!"

Just then Papa joined them. "Was this here before?"

"I don't think so." With nervous fingers Kate twisted the end of her braid, trying to think it through. "When I got the fire out, I walked around the house. I looked for anything I could find—anything that would show me who had been here. I wouldn't have missed these words."

Papa looked grim. "So whoever wrote them was here after you put out the fire?"

Kate's stomach was doing strange flip-flops. "He must have hidden in the trees. He watched me put out the fire. Then he came back."

"But why?" Anders asked. "Whoever it is could have started the fire again. Why didn't he?"

"Maybe he was going to," Papa answered. "Maybe we returned just in time."

"But if that's true, shouldn't I stay here and watch?" Anders asked.

"You could," Papa told him. "But we can't have someone here every hour of the day. We'd never get our work done. Besides, the minute we left, he'd try again."

Once more Papa looked down at the ground. "Whoever wrote these words has gotten his message across. Next time he'll strike somewhere else."

"Somewhere else?" The idea filled Kate with dread. "Where?"

"I don't know," Papa answered. "I wish I did."

"I think I know who that person is," Kate said. "It has to be Dugan!"

"Who's Dugan?" Papa asked.

As Kate explained what Ben had said, all her fear poured out. "Dugan told Ben he'd get even," Kate finished. "It looks like he has!"

"Did Ben say anything else?" Papa asked.

Kate looked up into his clear eyes. Suddenly she felt glad she could talk to her stepfather.

"Ben warned me," Kate answered. "He said Dugan hates him so much that he might try to get even through me."

Kate cleared her throat, made herself go on. "Ben said Dugan could do anything—even something crazy."

"I better make a trip into Grantsburg," Papa answered. "I'll have a talk with the sheriff. Maybe Charlie will know where to find Dugan."

As they rode back to Windy Hill, Papa looked at Kate curiously. "How did you happen to find the fire?"

"I like to take this path," Kate said. "I like to think about Ben and Jenny getting married and living here."

"It will take Ben longer now." Papa's face looked grim.

"All that hard work on the house—wrecked in just a few minutes!"

But then Papa's voice turned gentle. "Is there anything else bothering you, Kate?"

As though he were still speaking, Kate remembered Lars urging her to talk to Papa. Should she tell him about Windsong and Breeza acting up in Grantsburg? It had felt so good to tell Papa about Dugan. Maybe Papa would understand about the horses too.

When Kate explained how the horses had behaved at the blacksmith shop, Papa listened carefully.

"They acted up just when Dugan came around?" he asked.

"That's the only time. Ben said that Dugan whipped the horses."

"And we all know he didn't feed them right," Papa answered. For a few minutes he rode in silence, thinking about it.

"Lars is right," he finally said. "Horses do act different around different people. A strong-willed horse will obey a rider who knows what she's doing, but not someone else."

"So Lars can ride Windsong and Breeza?" Kate asked. "It's all right?"

"Tell you what," Papa said. "Why don't I ride Breeza into Grantsburg? It would give me a good chance to check him out."

Kate nodded. That was fair enough. And it felt good being honest with Papa.

"Tomorrow we'll take the honey off the hives," he said. "I want to get it before a bear does!"

———

The minute they reached home, Papa left to talk with Charlie Saunders. When Papa returned late that afternoon, he said that Charlie and Big Gust had promised to keep an eye out for Dugan. Yet Kate and everyone else knew that there were eleven miles of countryside between the sheriff, Big Gust, and them.

Papa also had good news for Kate. "If Windsong acts like Breeza, both of them are great horses. If Lars is careful, he can ride them. And so can you."

Tears of relief welled up in Kate's eyes. When she gave Lars permission to ride Breeza, his grin stretched across his face.

After supper, Kate, Anders, and Lars took out the three horses. As they rode bareback along the wagon road that led to Spirit Lake School, Kate talked to Windsong. Whenever Kate spoke, the mare twitched her ears, as if trying to listen.

The trail led them close to Rice Lake. On a stretch of firm ground near a large hill, Wildfire turned toward the water.

"Want to try swimming?" Anders asked. Wildfire was used to going into the small lake with Anders.

When Kate and Lars agreed, Anders urged Wildfire into the water. Kate followed on Windsong. Lars and Breeza stayed right behind.

As the water rose around Kate's legs, Windsong began swimming. Knowing she could slide off, Kate felt half-scared, half-excited. But then she saw Anders. Her brother was whooping and hollering, having the time of his life.

Watching him, Kate let the water lift her off Windsong's back. With one hand clutching the reins, she floated alongside the mare. With her other hand, Kate caught her fingers in Windsong's mane.

As the cool water washed over Kate's arms and legs, the heat of the day fell away. Even her memory of the fire at Ben's house seemed less terrible.

After swimming awhile, Anders and Wildfire turned toward shore. Windsong followed, and soon her hooves found the bottom of the lake. Once more Kate swung onto her back. Each time Windsong lunged forward, Kate rose with her. Again Kate felt scared, wondering if she were going to fall off. But now she was moving with the mare.

Still clinging to Windsong's mane, Kate reached land safely. Suddenly the mare shook herself like a dog. As water sprayed around her, Kate laughed with delight.

From Rice Lake, Anders led them back past the farmhouse. Whenever Kate moved a knee or foot, Windsong obeyed. If Kate moved her wrist even slightly, Windsong responded to the rein. Yet her head still drooped, as though she had no life.

Together Kate, Anders, and Lars took the trail through the woods to the main road. As the trees thinned out, Kate heard the steady beat of a drum.

Windsong lifted her head. Her ears turned toward the sound.

Then Kate heard other instruments. As the band music grew louder, the mare picked up her pace.

"Look at her!" Kate told the boys. She liked this spirited mare she was seeing for the first time. "Have you ever heard of a music-loving horse?"

"Aw, Kate—" Anders groaned.

"My imagination, huh? Well, it's not!"

On the road three young men came into view. One of them pounded a large bass drum. The second played a lively march on the trumpet. The third young man moved the long slide of his trombone in and out.

"Who are they?" Kate asked, as curious as always. It wasn't every day that three musicians walked down the road.

"Members of the Trade Lake Band," Anders told her. "I've seen 'em before. They practice on their way to rehearse with Mr. Peters."

Mr. Peters was Kate's organ teacher, and she knew him well. "Did you know people believe he's the best musician in all of Burnett County?" she asked.

Reining in, Anders waited for the young men to pass by. But Windsong and Breeza seemed to stand at attention.

"Kate, can I ride Windsong for a few minutes?" Lars

asked as the musicians marched beyond them. "I want to try something."

When Lars settled into Windsong's saddle, he stretched forward his left foot. Just back of the mare's front leg, Lars put pressure on her side.

Suddenly Windsong stretched out her right foreleg, taking an extra long step. As Lars put pressure behind the mare's right leg, Windsong stretched out her left foreleg, again taking a long step.

Kate laughed. "Windsong is dancing!"

"It's like I told you!" Lars exclaimed. "She can do tricks!"

"But how did you know the signal?" Kate asked.

"I watched the horse trainer at the circus. I wondered if Windsong knew the same cues."

"Did you try it on Breeza?" Kate asked.

"Yup. He doesn't know that trick. But he came alive with the music too. Maybe he knows things that Windsong doesn't know."

"Windsong has other tricks?" Anders asked.

"She bows," Kate told him.

"Aw, c'mon, Kate! She *bows*? Even in a circus it's unusual to teach tricks to a mare. Having a horse is going to your head!"

"But Windsong *did* bow!" Kate insisted. "She bent her forelegs beneath her!"

Without a word Lars slipped down from the mare and walked back into the trees.

"Where you going, Lars?" Anders called.

Soon the nine-year-old returned with a small stick in his hand. Gently he tapped the upper part of Windsong's front leg. Bending her forelegs beneath her, the mare dropped down on her knees.

Anders yelped. "She really does bow!"

Lars winked at Kate. Without doubt, they were friends again, and she felt glad.

"I keep wondering about something," Kate said as they rode back to the farmhouse. "Ben says Windsong and

Breeza belonged to Dugan. But why would a circus sell valuable horses?"

"Maybe it was a little circus that went out of business," Anders told her. "Maybe they had to sell to the first person who came along."

Each time she learned something new about the mare, Kate liked Windsong even more. Leaning forward, Kate wrapped her arms around the mare's neck.

"You're my horse, Windsong!" Kate whispered in her ear. "My very own horse! I just want you to be mine forever!"

When they reached the farm buildings, Kate opened the gate and let the mare through. Breeza followed Windsong into the barn, again going to Windsong's left. Wildfire walked into her usual stall, second from Windsong's right.

As Kate stood back, looking at them, the three horses seemed a special gift—a very unusual gift for young people their age. Yet for some reason that Kate couldn't explain, she felt uneasy.

11

What If?

*J*ust before sundown, Papa, Anders, and Grandpa quietly left the house. Walking toward the surrounding woods, each took a different direction. Kate felt sure that she knew what they were doing—keeping a watchful eye.

When they returned, Kate heard Papa and Mama talking. More than once the word *fire* passed between them.

Papa needed to give no more warning about fires. From the oldest to the youngest, they knew the danger of just one runaway spark. Each time Kate needed to light the farm lantern she went to a spot out of the wind. Whenever she lifted the glass globe to light the wick, she was careful. Always she felt relieved to set down the glass, closing in the flame.

"Tomorrow we'll take the honey off the hives," Papa said just before going to bed. "If we work hard, we'll get it all spun out and into jars in one day."

At breakfast the next morning it was already hot. Inside the summer kitchen, the temperature was even worse. Mama had started a small fire in the cookstove to make coffee.

The minute they finished eating, the family vanished—no doubt searching for cooler air. Only Papa and Mama remained. Kate stood near a window, washing dishes.

Outside, long grass curled over the edge of the hill. It was wheat-colored now from the heat and lack of rain. Between the summer kitchen and the barn lay the brown, dead-looking growth that Kate still called "Mama's grass."

As Kate rinsed the plates, she couldn't help thinking about the woods. Reddish brown needles covered the ground under each pine tree. Beneath the oaks and maples, dry leaves carpeted the earth.

Last autumn Kate had dragged her feet through those leaves, just to hear the rustle. Until this summer she had loved that sound. Now she knew the danger of the dry woods so close to the house.

"Before we take off the honey, I want to do something even more important," Papa said.

Kate turned in surprise. As she watched, Papa poured the hot coffee into his saucer.

"There's a Bible verse I keep thinking about," he said.

"Yah?" Mama answered. "What is that?"

"The one that says Noah did everything the Lord commanded him."

"What a strange verse!" Mama sat down at the table, giving Papa her full attention. "Why do you suppose God is reminding you of that?"

"An idea has come into my head several times," Papa said. "I believe it's something the Lord wants me to do."

As Mama listened, Kate saw her eyes. Round and large and blue, they seemed filled with questions.

"I need to plow around the buildings," Papa said. "I want a ten- or twelve-foot stretch of land without any grass or brush."

"For a firebreak?" Mama asked. "You think—" She stopped, as though not wanting to utter the words.

"I don't know." Papa blew on his coffee to cool it, but

his gaze never left Mama. "I just know I'm supposed to plow the ground."

"Yah?" A strange look flashed across Mama's face, as though she were trying to hide her fear.

"Ingrid," Papa said gently. "There's something else. I need to plow between the house and the barn."

"Oh, Carl!" It was the first time Kate had ever heard Mama object to something Papa said. "You worked so hard to grow that grass for me. We all carried water until we had to give up. But when it rains, it will come back. It will be green again."

"I know. That's why I want to tell you before I plow it. The grass is so dry that one tiny spark—"

"You've prayed about it?" Mama asked.

Papa nodded. "Many times." As though he hated even the thought of destroying Mama's grass, he covered her hand with his.

"You never complained about the long winter when I left for logging camp." Papa's voice was gentle. "You never complain about the hard work. It will be worse with the grass gone. If you really say no, I won't do it, because you listen to God too."

A long look passed between them. "It has been good grass," Mama said at last. "It has helped to keep the mud and the sand out of the house. But I give the grass to you."

For a moment longer Papa gazed into Mama's eyes. Leaning forward, he bent his head and kissed her on the cheek.

When Papa went outside, he hitched Windsong and Breeza to the plow. Then he found another harness and a plow for breaking sod. To that plow he hitched Dolly and Florie.

Anders went first with the big draft horses, and Papa followed with the other two. It was the first time Kate had watched her horses in harness, and they seemed willing to work.

On the east and west sides of the farm buildings the land

dropped away in steep hills. A hayfield, pasture, and crop-land lay on the north and east, and the oat field on the south.

Papa and Anders started there, plowing several rows to separate the house from the dry, brown field. Even Mama came outside to watch the soil being turned over.

As Mama went back to work, Papa and Anders plowed furrows in the side of the hill east of the house. Continuing on with their circle, Papa and Anders came to the far side of the barn.

Kate and Lars brought Wildfire and the cows inside, and Papa made an opening in the pasture fence. There he and Anders plowed another firebreak. Beyond the turned-over ground was the hayfield and the woods that led to Ben's house.

When the teams of horses reached the granary they had to stop. The building was perched too close to the edge of the steep hill for them to plow on the other side. Beyond the granary, Papa and Anders plowed again, completing the circle.

As Anders turned Dolly and Florie back to the barn, Papa stopped him. "We need to plow between the house and the barn."

His voice sounded heavy, and Kate knew that Papa had saved the dreaded job until last.

Anders looked at Papa in surprise. "Mama's grass?"

"I'm afraid so," Papa answered.

But Anders just stood there. "Will you take Dolly and Florie?" he asked, as though not wanting to start.

When they changed places, Papa directed the large draft horses to the edge of the grass. For a moment he glanced toward the house, as though wondering if Mama watched from inside. Then Papa set the plow in the ground and urged the horses ahead.

Anders followed with the other team. Before long, several furrows lay between the house and the barn.

In early spring Kate had liked seeing such furrows. Always they changed into newly planted ground. But now

Kate hated the turned-over earth. The furrows made her afraid.

When Papa and Anders finished plowing, they connected the fence again. Still working together, they rolled three large barrels to the edge of the hill next to the granary. While Grandpa pumped, the rest of them filled the barrels with water. Inside the granary door, Papa placed buckets and a pile of gunnysacks, ready for wetting down, if needed.

As Kate watched Papa's careful preparations, she felt glad that he wanted to do his best to protect them. At the same time Kate felt scared. Her stepfather was doing everything he could to save his buildings, if it came to that. Yet the back side of the granary—the only hole in the circle— might be the place where they needed a firebreak most.

With dread Kate remembered how often the wind blew from that direction. What if a fire started in the long, dry grass next to Rice Lake? In no time at all, the flames could sweep up the hillside. The house and summer kitchen, the granary and barn would all burn to the ground.

Kate shuddered. She tried to push the thought aside, but it would not leave her.

12

The Unwanted Visitor

$\mathcal{A}$s the family ate their noontime meal, Erik came to the summer kitchen. "Josie's father is ready to start threshing," he said.

"That changes everything," Papa told Mama. "I need to leave right away. That means the threshers will be here tomorrow."

The neighborhood farmers took turns helping one another by going from farm to farm. But Kate guessed what Papa was thinking. He was concerned about getting the honey off the hives.

As Erik sat down at the table, Kate gave him a plate filled with roast beef and potatoes. While Papa and Anders finished eating, Kate told Erik about the fire at Ben's house. When she described Dugan's threat to Ben, Erik scowled.

"Do you think Dugan creeps around the woods behind us?" Kate asked. "Do you suppose he watches whatever we do?"

"I don't know what else to think!" Erik exclaimed. "If Dugan sets fires—"

Erik looked at Papa. "What about the fire at Charlie's stable? Is there some reason Dugan would have set that?"

"Maybe he's against anyone in authority," Papa answered.

"Like a sheriff?" Kate asked.

Papa nodded. "Or *any* person who does the right thing."

"Like Ben," Kate said.

"Like Ben," Papa answered. He pushed back his plate.

"Ben told me Dugan wants money, and he's willing to steal for it." Kate pulled her long braid forward and nervously twisted its end. "If we knew what Dugan might try in order to get money—"

"We could catch him at it!" Erik exclaimed. "Maybe that's what happened—"

"With the tree that fell across the road!" Kate finished for him. "Do you think there's any connection?"

Erik grinned at Kate. "Are we wondering the same thing?"

Even now Kate hated to think about the man hiding behind the branches. As though reliving a bad dream, she saw his hand reach up to grab Windsong's bridle.

"But what did we have that was valuable?" Kate asked. "The horses? Would someone like Dugan sell his horses, then steal them back again?"

"It'd be quite a way to make money!" Anders broke in. "Selling the same horses over and over again. But you don't even know if you saw Dugan."

"I've been thinking about that," Erik said. "I'm pretty sure I saw something besides that big hat. When the man fell back, something waved—something that could have been a necktie."

"Hmmm." For Kate some pieces were falling together. "Ben said Dugan is a swell dresser. Sometimes he wore a necktie, even for work on the dam. Maybe he wants more money than he makes—money for clothes."

"Does Ben have any idea where Dugan is?" Erik asked.

"Nope," Kate told him. "Neither does Charlie. And Big Gust hasn't seen him either."

"Dugan has disappeared right off the face of the earth," Anders said. "I wonder where he'll show up next."

"Will you hitch Wildfire to the wagon before you go?" Mama asked Papa. "Kate and I need to use it."

Her stepfather's grin told Kate that the two of them had planned something special for her. As soon as Papa, Anders, and Erik were gone, Mama pulled off her apron.

"This afternoon we will buy cloth for your dress!" she announced.

"My dress for Ben's wedding?" Kate asked.

"Yah, sure," Mama answered. "I want to start sewing right away."

Kate's heart leaped. When she asked Jenny if her dress should be a certain color, the teacher had smiled. *"Why don't you wear something blue to match your pretty eyes?"*

Kate felt bubbly inside just thinking about Jenny's words. It was fun knowing that her teacher thought she had pretty eyes. Even more, Kate felt excited each time she thought about Ben and Jenny getting married.

"But what about the threshers coming tomorrow?" Kate asked Mama. Last year her mother had hurried around the kitchen for days, getting food ready.

"I will make the pies," Grandma said quickly.

Kate stared at her grandmother. She had never made pies in Sweden and had only learned since coming to America. Was Grandma just as eager as Mama for Kate to have a nice dress?

Before Papa left, he brought Wildfire to the hitching rail. Kate felt proud that Papa believed she could handle the horse and wagon.

On the dusty road to Trade Lake, Mama held little Bernie in her arms. For Kate it would be a special afternoon with her mother.

"What if we can't find the right cloth here?" Kate asked as she and Mama started up the steps of Gustafson's Mercantile Store.

"Then we'll try Trader Carlson's."

"What if they don't have blue?"

Mama smiled. "Then we'll go to Grantsburg on another day."

Windy Hill Farm was eleven miles from Grantsburg. "You would go all that way for just the right color?" It was hard to believe.

At the top of the steps Mama stopped. "This is your growing-up dress, Kate. I'm going to sew a dress for the young lady you've become."

Kate blinked. "Sometimes I don't act like a young lady."

"I know. That whistle of yours—" Mama shook her head in despair, then smiled. "But I guess you need to be able to call Windsong."

"I guess," Kate answered. She felt relieved that Mama understood.

At the shelves filled with cloth, Kate saw three shades of blue. Mama took each bolt of cloth and held it in front of Kate. She found one piece of cloth that was close, but Mama left the store without it. "It's not the color of your eyes," she told Kate as they walked down the street to Trader Carlson's.

For years Mama had sewn clothes for Kate, using left-over scraps from dresses for wealthy ladies. Never before had Kate seen her mother search out just the right color.

"Won't the cloth cost a lot?" Kate asked.

"I've been saving my egg money." Mama smiled as though sharing a secret. "Ever since Jenny came for Ben's birthday, I knew we'd have a match!"

At Trader Carlson's store Mama started the process all over again.

The longer they searched, the more Kate wondered if she truly would look grown-up when the dress was finished.

Finally Mama told the clerk, "I want the finest cloth I can buy. And blue besides! Are you sure you've shown me everything?"

"Well, there's one more bolt of cloth—" The woman took it out from under the counter.

Taking a corner, Mama crushed the cloth to test it for wrinkles. Then she lifted the material up beneath Kate's chin.

"Ahhhh," Mama said. "It is just the color of your eyes." Turning, she told the clerk the number of yards she wanted.

"Mama," Kate whispered. "You didn't ask the price."

"I know," her mother whispered back. "If she cuts the cloth first, I can't change my mind."

Kate giggled. But when Mama heard the price, she swallowed hard. Even so, she opened her purse without hesitation. Laying out the coins, she counted. After paying, she had one penny left.

"All your hard work, Mama!" Kate said as they left the store. "Day after day you collected eggs." Much as Kate wanted a beautiful dress for Ben's wedding, she felt concerned. "I hope the dress will be worth it."

"It will," Mama answered. "It's not just for Ben's wedding. It's also for *you*."

Deep in her being, Kate felt warmed by Mama's smile. It reminded Kate of a time when she was little. She had fallen down and scraped her knee, and Mama kissed the hurt away. Yet here was something more. Mama's love reached into the future.

All at once there was something Kate knew. *Mama really cares about what kind of woman I'll be.*

"Thanks, Mama," Kate said softly. "Thanks for the beautiful cloth—for the dress you'll make." Kate felt overwhelmed by that gift. Then she realized her mother had given her something even better.

"Thanks for this special time with you," Kate said.

———————

When they reached the trail leading into Windy Hill Farm, Kate stopped at the mailbox. She found a letter addressed to her. "It's from Ben!" she exclaimed when she saw the return address. "He must have written the minute he got back to work!"

Right there Kate opened the letter. She was surprised to find it was written on one of those new typing machines. Some of the letters were missing:

```
De r K te,

I  m in big trouble.  If Dug n wins,
no job, no wedding, no Jenny.  Ple se
 sk f mily to pr y for me.

                        Ben
```

"Ben says he's in big trouble," Kate said as she figured out the words with the missing letters. "He wants us to pray for him."

"Oh, dear!" Mama exclaimed. "What can be wrong?"

"Whatever it is, it must be awful," Kate answered. "Ben wouldn't write something like that unless he's really upset."

During the rest of the ride home, she and Mama talked about what could have happened.

When they reached the barn, Kate jumped down, tied Wildfire's lead rope to the hitching rail, then helped her mother and Bernie from the wagon. As Mama started toward the house, Kate glanced toward the hives.

Kate gasped. No longer did the hives stand tall and straight, filled with their wealth of honey. Tossed over, lying every which way, the hive boxes were scattered across the grass.

Sick at heart, Kate broke into a run.

13

No Matter What!

*A*s Kate drew near the hives, she stopped. An angry hum filled the air—bees upset about the destruction of their home. Afraid to walk too close, Kate moved slowly and quietly.

In the midst of the smashed hives, a few boxes stood on the ground, right side up. As though a mighty paw had swatted them through the air, they were three and four feet away from their usual place.

Other boxes were tipped over, broken, and scattered at every angle. Frames lay fanned across the ground. Any queen within them had probably been killed.

Ready to straighten things out, Kate forgot herself and stepped forward. In mass the bees rose from the frames. As their angry buzzing increased, Kate edged back, needing no other warning.

A trail of broken frames led off into the nearby trees. More frames and empty hive boxes lay beneath the bushes. There, too, were smashed frames, wet with honey. Spilled out, stepped on, matted into the grass, golden honey clung to everything.

Tears welled up in Kate's eyes. All of Papa's hard work! All the honey they needed for winter! The honey they needed to sell. The honey the bees needed to live.

Overwhelmed by the disaster, Kate looked down and her tears turned to anger. Near where she stood, a frame lay on the ground. A frame filled with honey and capped with beeswax. Across the honeycomb was the claw mark of a large bear.

———

When Papa saw the destruction, he shook his head. "Of all the times when Lutfisk needed to be here, it was today." Instead, the dog had followed Papa when he helped the neighbors with threshing.

The cleanup was as awful as Kate expected. Papa started by putting together the hive boxes that weren't broken. But Kate knew that even Papa's best attempts could cause a fight among the bees. If the right boxes weren't put together, one set of bees could attack another, even killing the queen.

In one pile Papa set the frames and boxes he would repair. In another he put everything damaged beyond fixing. When he finally closed up the last hive, his shoulders slumped with discouragement.

"There's no extra honey, is there?" Kate asked, though she knew the answer.

"I doubt if even the bees have enough for winter," Papa said. "And I don't know how many queens were killed."

When the bees were that upset, not even Papa was willing to search for the queen that should be in each hive.

"Worst of all," Papa said, "the bear will come back."

———

The next day neighboring farmers came to thresh the oats. One man fed bundles into the huge threshing machine. While straw spewed out a spout at one end, a chain with paddles carried the grain up to a bucketlike scale. From there the grain slid down a pipe. Some of the men bagged the grain, and others carried the sacks to the granary.

While Mama and Grandma prepared the meal in the hot summer kitchen, Kate set the large dining room table. As they worked together, Kate watched her mother and grandmother. *Will I ever be the kind of women they are?* she wondered.

When the threshers came to the house, each man stopped at the basin on a bench outside the door. As soon as everyone cleaned up, they gathered around the table.

Papa bowed his head. "We thank thee, Heavenly Father, that thou art the giver of the harvest. We thank thee that thou wilt make the harvest stretch far enough. We bless this food in thy name. Ah-men."

What a strange prayer! Kate thought as she carried the meat and potatoes in from the summer kitchen. What did Papa mean by making the harvest stretch far enough?

When the men finished Grandma's good pie and stood up again, Kate found out. That afternoon the threshers were going on to the Lundgren farm.

"So soon?" Kate asked Mama. "They've been here only one morning!"

"Yah," Mama said, as though she weren't surprised. "They are done threshing here."

"Done? Already? Last year—" Kate broke off, thinking about it.

Last year it had rained at just the right times. When the farmers came for threshing, the oats flowed into sack after sack.

In that moment Kate realized what she had done. "Oh, Mama! I bought two horses—not one, but *two*! Two horses that need extra oats!"

When her mother said nothing, Kate understood. Mama had known from the start that there would be a problem. Even when Kate brought the horses home, Mama had asked, "Papa thought it was all right?"

"Why did Papa let me buy two horses?" Kate asked.

"He knows that you and Anders are old enough to make

choices." Mama answered so quickly that Kate felt sure her parents had talked about it.

"But what if I don't make a good choice?" she asked. Much as she loved both horses, and especially Windsong, Kate couldn't help but wonder now.

"Then you have to live with that choice," Mama said. "That's part of growing up."

So I was right, Kate thought. *The shocks were too far apart, the heads of grain too small. And I didn't want to think about the harvest!*

Feeling as if she couldn't breathe, Kate hurried to the door.

"Just wait," Mama called after her, as though wanting to give all the hope she could. "Wait till you see what Papa says."

But Kate couldn't wait. She had to talk to Papa now. At the front of the house, away from the other men, she found him.

"Mama said you didn't get many oats," Kate blurted out.

"Yah, that is true," Papa answered simply. He looked away, across what had been the oat field, but Kate had seen his discouragement.

"Oh, Papa! I'm sorry that I bought two horses! Horses that need even more oats!"

Kate ached, just thinking about it. "I was trying to help you—to give you another team. I wanted—"

Kate stopped. *I wanted Erik to like me. I wanted him to have a horse he could use.*

"Papa—" Kate's lips felt stiff. She could barely ask the worst question of all. "Will there be enough oats?"

Her stepfather's gaze returned to her. "We'll make the oats stretch as far as we can."

"But you need seed for next year. You need oats for *us* to eat!"

"Yah, sure." Papa wiped his forehead with his big red handkerchief. "But we'll do our best to make things stretch.

Maybe next year there will be more rain."

Rain, Kate thought. *How could I be so selfish? I was so busy buying two horses, I forgot they needed to eat! I forgot what having extra horses would do to Papa!*

Turning, Kate hurried away. Not till she reached the spring at the bottom of the hill did she stop. There she knelt down and splashed water on her face. But Kate could not wash away her awful feelings.

When she sat up again, the cool water dripped onto her shoulders. Gazing out across Rice Lake, Kate remembered the thought she'd had in Charlie's stable. *If we don't stick together as a family, we won't make it.*

In the next instant Kate flipped her braid over her shoulder. *No matter what happens, I'm going to help my family. I'm going to do whatever it takes to stick together!*

14

Ben's Trouble

*T*hat afternoon Mama laid the blue cloth on the dining room table. Carefully she cut out Kate's dress.

"Mama, aren't you sorry that you bought such fine cloth?" Kate asked. "Don't you feel bad that you spent so much money?"

"No, Kate," Mama answered, and Kate knew her mother wouldn't look back. "I'm going to sew you a dress you'll remember the rest of your life."

To Kate's surprise Mama wouldn't allow her to take even one stitch in the fine cloth. Kate knew it wasn't because Mama thought she couldn't sew well enough. Often her mother had told Kate what a good seamstress she was. It was something more.

"This is your growing-up year," Mama explained. "Every girl needs to remember how it feels to become a young woman."

At the Lundgrens' farm there were even fewer oats to harvest. Instead of working late, Anders and Papa returned home in time for supper. As they entered the summer kitchen, Kate saw the look in their eyes. Erik's family was going to have a hard winter too.

After supper that night, Papa thanked God again for the harvest—for what they *did* get.

How can you pray that way? Kate wanted to ask. Even in the hardest times she had never heard Papa complain about God.

When Erik came over that evening, he and Anders, Kate and Lars went out to the barn. In the dim light the boys looked even more tan from working in the fields all day. As they sat down on kegs, Kate found a milking stool.

She dreaded what she had to tell them. "I've done an awful thing," she said.

Without speaking, the boys waited for Kate to explain. None of them could hide how they felt. Kate saw it in their eyes. She also knew how important the big workhorses were to the family.

"If Papa doesn't have enough oats for Dolly and Florie, how can I use what little there is for Windsong and Breeza?" Kate asked.

Anders sighed. "I don't want to tell you what to do."

"I need to sell the horses, don't I?" Kate asked. Even as she spoke, she wanted to cry out against what she was saying. *No, no, no!*

"Maybe I could sell Breeza, but not Windsong." Yet Kate knew that wouldn't be enough. In the long, cold winter ahead, the oat bin would be empty.

Suddenly Erik ripped the straw he was chewing from his mouth. Leaping up, he stalked over to a nearby window. For a time he stood there, staring out. Kate knew he was angry, perhaps more upset than she had ever seen him. But when he turned back, he looked her in the eyes.

"You're right, Kate," he said. "I don't know what else you can do. But before you sell the horses, let's get them looking better."

"Let's find out if they know more tricks," Lars said,

speaking for the first time. "If you could sell them to a circus, you might get more money."

"Good idea!" Anders exclaimed.

Once more Erik sat down on a keg. When he looked at Kate, his eyes showed his concern. "The longer you keep Windsong, the harder it will be to say goodbye," he warned.

"I know," Kate told him. "It hurts just to think about it."

She stood up and walked into Windsong's stall. Leaning close, Kate whispered in the mare's ear. "I love you, girl."

As if in agreement, the horse gave a playful nudge with her nose.

Aching inside, Kate stroked Windsong's neck. "She's gentle with me," Kate told the boys. "She obeys as if she wants to please me."

"It's like her personality fits yours," Erik said.

"That's good, isn't it?" Kate asked.

"You betcha!" For the first time that evening Anders grinned. "Whenever someone can get along with you, it's good!"

Kate knew he was trying to help her feel better. She tried to laugh, but couldn't manage. Instead, she told the boys, "You're right, all of you. I don't have any choice but to sell the horses."

From that moment on the work began. Whenever they had even a few minutes of free time, Kate and the boys headed for Windsong and Breeza. When not grooming them, they tried to figure out what the horses knew. Because of his time with the horse trainer, Lars could figure out more than any of them. While in the barn one day, he decided that Breeza was a liberty horse.

"Do you remember that liberty act at the circus?" he asked Kate. "There was a lady with a long whip. She never used it on the horses, but it seemed to be a signal. When she cracked the whip or moved her hand a certain way, the horses obeyed."

Kate remembered all right. It had been a stunning act with a dozen white horses.

"But Windsong and Breeza are a different color," Kate said.

"Maybe all the horses were black except Breeza," Lars answered.

"The horses we saw seemed to know how to count!" Kate exclaimed.

One by one they had lined up in order, according to a large number on their back. Just before the finale, the woman blindfolded the last horse. Even with the blindfold, he ran around the ring, then took exactly the right place in the middle of the line.

"Why do you think Breeza was a liberty horse?" Kate asked. "Don't a lot of horses take a certain position because of the way they're hitched?"

Then she remembered. Even the first night, Breeza had chosen his own stall. Lars had also noticed how Breeza always went to Windsong's left.

Now he said, "Let's try something."

As Lars tied a blindfold over Breeza's eyes, Kate led Windsong outside.

"Ready?" Lars shouted.

Kate slapped Windsong on the rump. As the mare ran around the fenced-in area, Lars let Breeza out of the barn. Though blindfolded, he ran straight toward Windsong and the mare's left side.

Kate laughed. "You're right! How does Breeza do it?"

"By smell, I think," Lars said. "In a liberty act that's how horses know where to go. It looks like a horse is finding his number. But they just line up in the order they have in the stable."

"So Breeza is trained to find Windsong?" Kate asked.

Lars grinned. "Yah, sure, you betcha!" He sounded just like Anders.

On another day Kate and Lars discovered a trick by accident. As Kate slid to the ground after riding Windsong, a white handkerchief fell from her pocket. Kate didn't notice that she'd lost it, but Breeza did. He picked up the hankie in his teeth and brought it to Kate.

That success reminded her of something. At Charlie's stable and then at Ben's house, Windsong had nodded as if saying yes. When Kate told Lars about it, he asked, "What did you say to Windsong just before she moved her head?"

Kate thought back. She couldn't remember her words at Grantsburg. But at Ben's house—

Reaching up, Kate stroked the mare between her eyes. "You'll *help* me, won't you?" she asked.

In the next instant Windsong nodded as if answering.

"That's it!" Lars cried.

Again Kate stroked Windsong between the eyes, saying the word *help*. When the mare responded, Kate rewarded her with carrots.

On still other days, Kate practiced the signals Lars had shown them at Rice Lake. When Kate put pressure behind Windsong's right foreleg, the mare stretched out her left leg in an extra long step. When Kate gave the cue on Windsong's left side, the mare extended her right foreleg, again in an extra long step.

By now the horses had started to look better. They weren't sleek yet, but not as shaggy either. Windsong's ribs still showed, but not as much. Whenever Kate gave out oats, she measured carefully, thinking about the winter ahead.

The more time she spent with Windsong, the more Kate dreaded the moment when she had to give her up. It wasn't the tricks that meant the most to Kate, or even the possible value of the horses. She had learned to love both horses, and especially the mare.

Often Kate thought about the shadow outside the barn. Though she tried to push it away, a nagging thought remained. *What if Dugan steals Windsong and Breeza?* If that happened, Kate would lose both ways. Not only would the horses be gone. She wouldn't be able to buy the oats her horses had eaten.

As one week, then a second week passed, Kate grew

more hopeful. "Maybe Dugan has gone away for good," she said to Anders. "Maybe he's forgotten his grudge against Ben." Yet when Kate let down her guard, she felt uneasy.

Each morning the family prayed for rain and for Ben. Whenever they prayed, Kate wondered why Ben had sent such a letter. What was going on?

Then one evening Ben finally came home. This time Jenny wasn't along, and Kate wondered about it. While eating supper, Ben picked away at his food. Since he usually ate even more than Anders, Kate felt sure that whatever was wrong wasn't better yet.

"I'm really sorry about the damage to your house," Papa said. "But I think I know a way to fix it."

Papa had written to Ben after the fire. Yet to Kate's surprise Ben didn't want to know more about it.

"How is it going at Nevers Dam?" Mama asked, as though trying to get Ben to talk.

But Ben just shrugged. "Keep praying," he said.

Soon Kate noticed that Grandpa and Grandma were also watching Ben. It seemed as though the light had gone out of his eyes. What could be wrong?

When everyone finished eating, Ben said he needed to work on his house. From the window of the summer kitchen Kate watched Ben stop in the granary for his tools. Kate felt sure it was his love for Jenny that kept him working such long hours. Yet as Ben headed toward his house, his steps dragged.

As soon as Kate finished the dishes, she saddled Windsong and followed her uncle. When she reached the house, she found Ben hewing a log—chipping one side to make it flat.

Standing on top of the log, Ben walked backwards. Every four inches he struck the right side with a big broad ax. *Whack! Whack!* Yet he moved as though his heart wasn't in his work.

"What's the matter?" Kate asked.

As Ben dropped down on a stump, Kate found a place

on the grass beside him. The last time she had seen him here, he and Jenny glowed with excitement. Why did he look so discouraged now?

For a time Ben sat without speaking, staring down into the creek. When he finally started to talk, his voice was low, almost ashamed. "Do you remember when I told you about Dugan—the man I had to report?"

Kate nodded. "He said he'd get even with you."

"He's been gone for over a month now." Ben jumped up and paced around the open area near his house. "But money has been missing!"

"Missing! What do you mean?" Kate wasn't sure that she understood.

"Dugan left. He's nowhere to be found. But since I started working in the office—" Ben pounded his fist.

As though knowing what was coming, Kate felt butterflies in her stomach.

"Two times money has been missing!" Ben exclaimed. "After the first time, the boss talked to me."

Ben looked away, as if unable to meet Kate's gaze. "Mr. Frawley said, 'Ben, you're a good worker. I want to trust you, but you're the only person who is a watchman and works in the office too.'"

In front of Kate, Ben stopped pacing. "How did my boss know I was a thief? I haven't told *anyone* except our family and Jenny!"

"He accused you of stealing?" Kate asked.

Ben shook his head. "He said, 'I want to trust you.'"

Kate couldn't bear the idea of her special uncle being called a thief. But why would Mr. Frawley talk about trust unless he wondered about Ben's honesty?

"Maybe he talked that way without knowing what you did in Sweden," Kate answered, trying to offer hope.

As Ben dropped back on the stump, he ran his fingers through his hair. "Last week more money was missing. Mr. Frawley talked to me again! He said, 'Ben, we have to get to the bottom of this.' He thinks I stole the money!"

"Did he say so?"

Ben shook his head. "But who else could do it? I *know* that Mr. Frawley thinks I did!"

"But, Ben, you didn't!"

The tall young man tried to smile. "*I* know I didn't. And *you* know I didn't. But what about my boss?"

Ben's voice broke. "What about my Jenny? When we became friends, I told her I had been a thief in Sweden. I promised her I would never steal again. How can my Jenny marry someone with the name of a thief?"

Tears welled up in Kate's eyes. "Oh, Ben!"

As though Jenny were still standing there, Kate could see her looking up into Ben's happy face. As if Mama were still buying the blue cloth, Kate remembered her costly choice. She remembered all the happy preparations Mama and Grandma were making for the wedding.

But the blue dress and the work weren't important. All that mattered was what would happen to Jenny and Ben. If Ben's name wasn't cleared, there would be no wedding. Even if Jenny believed in him, Ben would never marry her while being called a thief.

This time it was Kate who jumped up. "That awful Dugan is getting even! We have to find him!"

For a moment Ben's eyes lit with hope. Then he moaned. "But where *is* Dugan? I never see him! I watch the woods. I watch the road past the office. I only know that he's been there! How can we catch someone we cannot see?"

Again Kate remembered her uneasiness about Windsong and Breeza. She had never been able to completely forget that shadow—that thud outside the barn.

"If Dugan is still around—" Kate thought about it. "There's one link between you and us and Dugan," she said slowly. "It's the horses!"

Standing taller, Kate flipped her braid over her shoulder. "We'll find Dugan before he wrecks your good name!"

"Before Dugan steals again?" Ben asked, his voice quiet but desperate. "Before my Jenny gets hurt?"

15

Where's Papa?

"*Before* your Jenny gets hurt!" Kate exclaimed.

"How?" Ben's gaze met hers. "How can you stop Dugan?"

"I don't know, Ben." Kate wished she could offer more comfort. "But somehow we will."

"You promise?"

"I promise. I don't know how, but we will."

When Kate returned to Windy Hill Farm, Mama asked if she would watch Bernie for a while. Taking the baby with her, Kate searched out Anders. She found him in the summer kitchen. Together they talked about Dugan and Ben.

"What can we do?" Kate asked, feeling as desperate as Ben had sounded.

But Anders didn't have any more ideas than she did. Finally Kate had to give up trying to think of a plan. She felt hot and tired and discouraged.

"Take Bernie, will you?" she asked Anders.

Since the birth of her baby brother, Kate had wanted to see Anders hold him. But when he tried to settle the baby,

Anders seemed all arms and big hands.

"Here," Kate said, rescuing Bernie. "I'll show you what he likes."

Holding her little brother up on her shoulder, she patted his back until he burped. Then she sat down next to Anders. With Bernie in her lap, she cradled his head in her hands. "If you hold him so he sees your face, he'll talk to you."

"Talk!" Anders scoffed. "How can a five-month-old baby talk to anyone?"

"You'll see," Kate answered. Once more she handed Bernie over.

Anders still looked awkward, but this time he held the baby on his legs, cradling the small head in his big hands. Gazing up at Anders, Bernie gurgled and smiled.

Anders grinned. Before long, he was making funny sounds with his tongue, clucking as though he'd talked with Bernie all his life.

"Look!" Anders exclaimed. "See how he's laughing?"

Kate smiled. Already Anders had forgotten his awkwardness.

"He likes me!" Anders took Bernie off his knees and cradled him in his arms. "I have a way with babies, all right!"

Moments later, Bernie started fussing. For a few minutes Anders jiggled Bernie up and down, the way Kate often did.

Suddenly Anders shifted the baby. A wet spot darkened his shirt.

"Oh, yuck! He wet his pants!"

As Kate giggled, Anders passed Bernie off to her. While Kate changed her little brother, Anders picked up an old issue of the Frederic *Star*.

Just then Erik came to the door. When Kate gave him the last piece of apple pie, Erik sat down near Anders at the table.

Soon Anders looked up from the newspaper. "Kate, here's something for you!"

He began reading aloud. " '*The Charming Woman* is not necessarily one of perfect form and features.' "

Kate sighed. Anders had been so much better lately. She had really thought he was changing. But now he had found another way to torment her.

"Hear that, Kate?" Anders tipped back in his chair and looked over the newspaper.

"I hear you." She pretended she didn't care what Anders said.

But her brother read on: " 'Many a plain woman who could never serve as an artist's model has those rare qualities that all the world admires—' "

Kate looked down, but listened to every word. *That's what I want to be. A bridesmaid that everyone thinks is beautiful—especially Erik. What would all the world admire?*

" 'Neatness, clear eyes, clean smooth skin,' " Anders read. "Let's see, do you have that, Kate? Especially clean smooth skin?"

Kate slipped a dry shirt over Bernie's head. Not for anything would she answer, but her hand trembled.

" 'A physically weak woman is never attractive, not even to herself.' Well, that's for sure!"

Anders grinned at Kate. "Now, there's one thing you aren't, and that's physically weak. You can climb a tree faster than anyone—and swing on a rope in the hayloft—and what else can you do?" Anders paused and seemed to think about it.

"Now and then she gets the best of you." Erik's voice was soft, but there was no mistaking what he was trying to do.

Kate glanced up, grateful for someone who took her part.

But Anders returned to the newspaper: " 'Electric Bitters restore weak women, give strong nerves, bright eyes, smooth, velvety skin, beautiful complexion.' "

Quickly Kate put Bernie down in his cradle. She had no doubt where this was headed, and she wanted to escape while she could.

But Anders was faster. "That's what you need, Kate—

Electric Bitters." He leaned toward her. "My dear sister, is that a blemish I see on your forehead?"

A hot blush rose to Kate's face. If there was anything she didn't want Erik to notice, it was exactly that.

Like a newly kindled fire, Kate's temper flared. "How can you be so awful?" she asked.

Her brother grinned. "You want to be a strrrong woman! With strrrrong nerves! You can buy all the help you need at the drugstore. For only fifty cents!"

Kate's anger spilled over. "Strong nerves, all right!"

She flipped her long braid over her shoulder. "Having you for a brother is so terrible that I get stronger every day! For that you can watch Bernie!"

Without another word, she ran from the kitchen. Her brother's laughter followed her.

Kate fled to the house and the quiet of her bedroom. Through the open windows she heard Grandma enter the summer kitchen and take Bernie. Kate waited until Anders and Erik left. Then in the long summer evening, she finally came out of her room.

As she passed through the kitchen, Kate lit a lantern and carried it to the barn. When she reached Windsong's stall, she hung the lantern on a nail in the log beam overhead.

In times like this, Windsong seemed even more of a special friend. Kate felt sure the mare understood how she felt. When she buried her face in the horse's mane, Windsong craned her head, as if to offer comfort.

Slowly, carefully, Kate brushed out the horse's tail and mane. Windsong's coat looked so much better. Soon it would be satin smooth, Kate knew. And the mare's ribs no longer showed.

Before long Mama called, and Kate hurried from the barn into the dusk. By the time she went to bed that night, a strong breeze blew off Rice Lake. After the heat of the day, the wind offered a welcome change. Kate opened every window, then slipped into the bed she shared with Tina.

As Kate lay there, she listened to the wind stirring the

trees. *Maybe it'll be cooler tomorrow,* she thought with relief. With a branch tapping against the house, Kate fell asleep.

———————

As if from a distance, Kate heard a dog barking. Rolling over, she tried to push the sound away. But the dog kept barking.

Through the fog of sleep, Kate realized that the sound came from somewhere outside. It had to be Lutfisk. Yet Kate had seen Anders put the dog in the kitchen. What was bothering him?

For a moment Kate lay there, coming to. Still Lutfisk barked, now from farther away. Then, above the barking dog, Kate heard the bawling of cows. Something was wrong.

Rolling over, Kate opened her eyes and looked toward the windows. A strange orange light filled the night sky.

Kate jerked wide awake. In the next instant she leaped from bed to lean out the window. The barn was on fire!

Within seconds Kate pulled on her dress. Even in her panic, she moved without a sound, trying not to waken Tina. Moments later, Kate slipped from the room and pulled the door shut behind her.

At the bedroom where Mama and Papa slept, Kate pounded on the door, then opened it. "Fire in the barn!" she cried.

Without waiting for them to answer, Kate leaped down the stairs. Again she pounded on a door, this time for Grandpa and Grandma.

"Fire!" Kate cried again. "Fire in the barn!"

Each time she gave the warning, the nightmare seemed more real. Passing through the kitchen, Kate heard Papa behind her. Outside, she called into the summer kitchen for Ben, Anders, and Lars.

"Run to Erik's for help!" Papa told the nine-year-old.

Papa and Ben headed for the barn with Grandpa limping along behind. As they ran through the nearest doorway, flames leaped up the log wall.

Kate raced to the pump, then remembered the barrels on the edge of the hill. Already Anders had grabbed buckets and gunnysacks from the granary.

"Get the rest of the buckets!" he yelled, and Kate fled to the house.

By the time she returned, Mama was dipping water from one of the barrels. As she passed the pail to Grandma, Kate stepped into line. Taking the bucket from Grandma, Kate ran to Anders. Standing closest to the barn, he flung water at the fire.

On the east end and the side toward the house, flames covered the logs. A short distance away, Anders set a ladder against the wall. When he tried to pour water on the fire, he was forced back by the heat.

As Anders dropped to the ground, Kate saw his singed hair. When she passed another bucket, Anders threw the water as high as he could. Yet it didn't reach the flames. Tongues of fire licked the edge of the roof.

"It's burning so fast!" Kate cried. Already flames crept through the cracks between logs.

Inside the barn, horses whinnied. Cows bawled with terror. Pigs squealed above the roar of the blaze.

Soon the barrels at the edge of the hill were empty. When Mama ran to the rain barrels next to the house, Grandma and Kate followed. Once again they formed a line with full buckets moving toward Anders, empty ones coming back.

Even from where Kate stood she felt the intense heat.

"Don't spill!" Anders warned as he took a pail from her. Using each precious drop, he flung the water at the flames.

Coughing and choking, Ben appeared in the door closest to the pump. Using a large board, he tried to push a sow and her babies out of the barn.

Papa was next, chasing another squealing pig. In the light of the fire, sweat poured down Papa's face.

Quickly he tied a cloth across his mouth and nose. For

a moment he talked to Anders. Then Papa ran back into the barn. When Ben and Grandpa followed him, Anders chased the pigs farther away from the barn. Running every which direction, they zigzagged around him, trying to return to their pens.

As Anders struggled to keep them from the door, Kate flung the next bucket of water at the fire. Like a hungry beast, the flames leaped across the roof, feeding on the wooden shingles.

By now the rain barrels were empty, and Mama started pumping. Each time a bucket was full, Grandma passed it to Kate. Along the ridgepole, wind caught the fire, pushing the flames.

"The horses!" Kate cried, as the fire spread to the west end. She wanted to run inside, to lead Windsong from the barn before it was too late.

Instead, Grandpa and Ben brought out more pigs. The sows and piglets milled around, blocking the entrance.

Tears streamed from Papa's eyes as he chased out the next sow. Coughing from smoke, he called to Anders. "Get 'em farther away!"

Pushing and shoving, Anders and Grandpa herded the pigs where they could not return to the barn. With each bucket that came to her, Kate threw water toward the fire. As flames leaped closer, she stumbled back, coughing.

Cows were next, with their calves alongside. They, too, tried to go back into the barn. As Papa and Ben brought them out, Grandpa and Anders led the cows to the pasture. At a hole in the barbed wire, they pushed the animals through, then blocked the opening.

Snapping and crackling, flames leaped from a hole in the roof. Fire raced through the hay in the loft. Through an open door, Kate saw what was happening. Clumps of hay fell from the loft, lighting more hay on the ground below.

"Hurry!" Kate cried. As she waited for the next bucket, a section of roof fell in—the roof over where the pigs had been.

When Mama could pump no more, Kate hurried to take her place. Anders was ahead of her, pumping as he had never pumped before. Beneath his strong hands, the pump groaned and creaked.

Then Erik was there, and his father and older brother, John. In spite of the awfulness of the fire, Kate felt better just knowing Erik had come.

Moments later, Kate saw Lars. As he raced for the barn, Kate yelled at him. "Where are you going?"

"To help Grandpa!"

"No!" Kate warned him. "Don't ever go into a burning building!"

When Lars kept on, Kate ran after him. "Stop!" she cried. "Only a grown-up knows what to do!"

Grabbing his shirt, Kate pulled Lars into line next to her.

Once more Kate started passing buckets. On down the line the full bucket went to Mr. Lundgren. Empty buckets came back.

Without losing the rhythm, Erik took Anders' place at the pump. As soon as Erik filled a bucket, Kate handed it to Lars. With each pail he took, Kate felt grateful. At least she knew where he was.

Whenever Kate passed a pail, she looked toward the barn. By now, flames swallowed up the entire roof. With the wind fanning the blaze, the fire seemed to be everywhere at once.

As Kate passed another bucket, Erik's brother, John, ran to the door at the west end of the barn.

"At last—they'll bring out the horses!" Kate exclaimed.

A frightened whinny reached her ears. Kate's heart flip-flopped. "Is that Windsong?" she asked Erik. Neither of them were sure.

Again the horse whinnied, and a second horse answered. Trying not to hear, Kate covered her ears with her hands. Yet the cries of the animals still reached her. She could not shut out the sound.

Then another bucket was full. As Kate took it, water sloshed over her hands.

"Watch it, Kate!" Erik warned. "Don't lose a drop."

Up, down, up, down, the handle went. Without a pause, the pump poured out bucket after bucket of water.

In the light of the fire, a horse appeared, led out by John Lundgren. A gunnysack was over its head, but Kate knew it was Dolly. Grandpa reached up to grab the halter and led the frightened horse away from the barn. Across Papa's newly plowed ground he limped, taking the horse to safety.

As Ben came out with Florie, Anders ran toward the barn and grabbed the halter. The large draft horse fought against him, but Anders hung on and led Florie away. Then John brought out Wildfire.

Just then, at the opposite end of the barn, part of the loft caved in. Flames shot upward. Charred boards fell to the ground below.

With a gunnysack over Breeza's head, Ben was next in coming out. As Grandpa led the horse away, Kate watched for Windsong. Still, she saw no sign of the mare.

But now a new worry overwhelmed Kate. "Papa!" she cried. "Where is Papa?"

Frantic with fear, she ran to Anders. "You've got to go after him!"

Her brother's face was covered with soot. In the strange orange light Kate saw his eyes.

"Papa told me to stay outside, no matter what. If I have to, I'm supposed to get Mama and the rest of you away."

Then Kate knew. Papa wasn't just concerned about the barn. He was worried about the house, and all of them. He was worried about Bernie and Tina and whoever would be trapped if the flames leaped the firebreak. He was worried about the fire racing across the dry fields and through the dry woods.

"But where's Papa?" Kate cried again. "Where *is* he?"

16

The Forgotten Lantern

*U*p and down the line the question went, along with the buckets of water. With each pail that Kate passed, she looked toward the barn.

Like a skeleton, rafters stood against the night sky. With a shower of sparks, the middle of the loft fell in. The section near the horse stalls.

A cold fist tightened around Kate's heart. Would Papa lose his life over Windsong? As much as she loved the horse, Windsong wasn't worth that.

"Papa!" Kate cried again. "Where are you?"

Then, through the haze of smoke, Papa stumbled from the west end of the barn.

Behind Kate, Anders shouted with relief. "He's out!"

An instant later, the last part of the loft collapsed. Dark with smoke and soot, Papa staggered toward them.

"Carl!" Mama broke away from the bucket line. When she reached Papa, she threw her arms around him.

"I'm all right! I'm all right!" Papa exclaimed, and Mama returned to the bucket brigade.

As though set free, flames shot upward. Cinders sprayed out, driven by the wind.

"The house!" Kate yelled. "The summer kitchen!"

As sparks leaped the firebreak, one of them settled near the granary. In the dry grass close to the building, a flame caught and held.

Filled with panic, Kate remembered the oats stored in the granary. Grabbing a gunnysack, Kate soaked it in the next bucket of water and raced toward the granary. Using the wet sack, she pounded the ground.

Nearby, men yanked off their shirts and came to help.

"The roof!" someone shouted.

Anders ran for the ladder, set it against the side of the granary, and climbed up. When he reached the roof, he stayed there, pounding out the sparks that fell on the wooden shingles.

In the next minute a ring of watchful people formed a circle around the barn. Standing outside Papa's firebreak, they worked with feverish haste, pouncing on every spark that leaped beyond the plowed ground.

Unwilling to let one cinder get past her, Kate stayed near the granary. Even the walls were hot to her touch. The paint had blistered from the heat of the fire.

Gone were the doors of the barn, the loft, the hay that Papa had stored away for winter. At the west end, the log walls still stood. But on the east end where Kate first saw the fire, the walls were completely gone.

As men sloshed water against the large logs, Kate stared at the charred timbers. Then, through a haze of weariness, she felt a drop of rain.

At first the drops were gentle, splatting against the red-hot wood. Then the rain settled into a steady downpour—a rain so welcome that everyone stayed outside, hands lifted up, soaking it in. The rain they prayed for had come.

Their backs wet with rain and sweat, men stood around the barn, watching what was left of the fire.

"It's too late!" Kate moaned as Erik came to stand beside her.

"No!" he exclaimed. "It came in time to save the other buildings!"

Her knees too weak to stand any longer, Kate sank to the ground. In every bone and muscle she ached. Yet the fire had not spread to the woods or the other buildings. Papa's firebreak had held!

As Kate heard Bernie's cry, Mama ran past her. Moments later, Mama came back out of the house. A blanket protected little Bernie from the rain. Mama held him against her chest as if she would never let him go.

"Kate, where's Tina?" Mama asked.

Kate leaped to her feet. When she discovered the fire, Kate had left her sister in bed. *What if Tina woke up? What if she stumbled down the steps and out of the house? What if none of us saw her and she went too close to the fire?*

By the time Kate reached the second-floor bedroom she was out of breath. Quietly she opened the door. On tiptoes she crept toward the bed and leaned down. In the dim light from the window she saw Tina's face. With blond hair spread across the pillow, the little girl lay there, still fast asleep.

In spite of her tiredness, Kate flew down the stairs and found her mother.

"Tina's all right!" Kate said. "She's still sleeping."

As though unable to believe that anyone could sleep through such panic, Mama shook her head. "Thank you, God!" she exclaimed.

Near Mama stood a wet and dirty Lutfisk. Looking up at Kate, he wagged his tail and woofed. When he barked a second time, she remembered.

"That's what woke me up! Lutfisk was barking! How did he get out of the kitchen?"

Kate hurried back to the house. This time she saw what she had missed before. On the window closest to the door, the screen was ripped off.

"Do you think Lutfisk jumped through?" Kate asked when she returned to Mama.

Her mother was sure of it. In spite of her weariness, Mama smiled. "Lutfisk is making up for missing the bear. This time he warned us."

As Kate walked across the plowed ground, the big logs still glowed red, in spite of the rain. Papa, Anders, and Erik stood near the charred walls. When Anders saw Kate coming, he stopped talking.

In the first streaks of dawn he spoke quickly to the others. As they turned toward Kate, Papa and Erik fell silent.

Kate's fear changed to dread. "Where's Windsong?" she asked. All through the endless night, she had not seen the mare.

It was Papa who told Kate the bad news. "I don't know what happened to her," he said. "I've asked Ben and John because they helped me with the horses."

Papa's eyes showed his concern for Kate. "When I saw Windsong wasn't outside, I went back in to find her. A timber fell and hit my head."

In the early morning light Kate saw Papa's singed hair. In that moment Kate realized how much she loved her stepfather. Yet she didn't want to hear his words.

"I had to leave." Papa's voice broke. "I didn't have any choice."

Reaching out, he put his arm around Kate's shoulders. "I'm sorry, Kate. I'm really sorry, but I think Windsong is dead."

"It's not true!" Kate cried, shaking free from Papa's arm. "Windsong escaped!"

"Do you think so?" Anders asked, as if wanting to believe the mare was safe.

"She untied her rope before," Kate said. "She did it again."

"Which way did you tie it?" Anders asked.

Kate bit her lip. Though she didn't want to face the truth, she remembered. "The second way you taught me." Kate's voice was low with pain. "The way you said no horse on earth could untie."

Anders groaned. But when he looked at Papa, Kate knew there was something else.

"What is it?" Kate asked. "What do you know that I don't?"

"Even if Windsong got out, she wouldn't stay out," her brother said.

Kate stared at him. "She wouldn't stay out of a *fire*? She would go back into a burning barn?"

Anders nodded. "Even if the barn was falling in, Windsong would try to find her stall."

Kate was horrified. "But why?" She had seen the struggle Anders and Grandpa had with the cows and pigs. She had noticed the gunnysacks over the horses' heads. Yet she never dreamed it had anything to do with Windsong.

"Why?" Kate asked again. "Why do scared animals go back into a barn?"

"That's their home," Anders said. "That's the place they're most familiar with."

"Oh, Anders, I'm sick of your jokes! How can you tease about something like Windsong being dead?"

"I'm not teasing, Kate," he said quietly.

Kate turned to Erik. "Anders is lying, isn't he?"

When Erik shook his head, Kate asked again, "Erik?" Kate felt as if she were pleading for Windsong's life. "Is Anders really telling the truth?"

"I'm afraid so," Erik said, and Kate heard the grief in his voice. "I'm sorry, Kate, but Anders is right."

"No!" Kate cried. "You're wrong! You're both wrong!"

She turned to her stepfather. "Papa, tell me they're wrong!"

"I'm sorry, Kate," Papa said. "But the boys are right."

Kate swallowed hard. "So even if Windsong managed to untie herself, to open the gate again—she would have gone back in?"

Papa nodded. "I'm afraid so."

Suddenly Kate felt like a rock falling into a deep well. All through the terror of fighting the fire, she had tried to ignore her worry. As great sobs ripped through her being, Kate fled to the house.

No longer could she push one memory aside. *I forgot the lantern. I left the lantern in the barn!*

17

What's Worse?

*T*he news about the burned-down barn traveled quickly, spread by word of mouth from farm to farm. All that day people came to help Papa. One man brought a load of hay. Another carried barbed wire to build a fenced-in area for the animals. A third had an extra harness along. And everyone brought food.

One neighbor after another sought out Kate. "I'm sorry about your horse," they would always say.

"I am too," Kate answered. Each time she looked toward the skeleton timbers and broken walls of the barn, she wanted to cry out, "It's my fault! It's my fault!" Like a giant hand, a fist tightened around her heart.

By afternoon Kate could no longer stand her thoughts. Escaping into the woods, she took the trail to Ben's house. Without Windsong, the walk seemed to last forever.

As Kate sat down on the bank overlooking the creek, tears welled up, blurring her vision. With the rain of the night before, the water ran higher, but she barely noticed. *I burned down the barn. I killed my own horse!*

There, beside the creek, she thought back to the day

when she bought Windsong and Breeza. *I wanted to help my family. I wanted Erik to think I'm really special.*

But now everything had turned into a nightmare. *If Papa finds out what I did, he'll hate me. If Erik knows, he'll never want to see me again. And Anders! Anders would never let me live this down! For the rest of my life I would hear about setting the barn on fire!*

Everything came back to one thought. *It's my fault.*

Tormented by worry, Kate again started weeping. As sobs shook her body, she cried until no more tears came.

When at last she drew a long gasping breath, Kate heard a sound behind her. Turning, she saw Erik not far away.

"I didn't want to scare you," he said as he sat down beside her.

Suddenly self-conscious, Kate pushed back the hair that had fallen into her face. "I'm an awful mess!"

Erik grinned. "No you aren't. You look as pretty as always."

Kate's heart leaped, but she found it hard to believe him. "With red eyes? And blotchy skin?"

Reaching into a pocket, Kate found a hankie and blew her nose. In spite of how awful she looked, she was glad Erik was here.

For a time he sat without speaking, and Kate felt grateful for his silence. "Thanks, Erik," she said at last.

"For nothing?" Again he smiled, but his eyes showed his hurt for her.

"Thanks for caring," Kate said. "For caring about Windsong." As she spoke the name, the mare's death seemed real again.

Grief tightened Kate's throat. "It's so hard to look ahead," she said finally. "Until we talked about selling her, I thought she'd always belong to me. I thought that over the years we'd grow to know each other and be—" Kate stopped, unable to go on.

"Best friends?" Erik asked.

Kate nodded. "And now my dreams are gone."

"All of them?" Erik asked.

The question surprised Kate. "No, not all of them," she said slowly. "I still want to be a great organist. I want to be a music teacher. I want to help other people like music the way I do."

"You have big dreams." Erik waited.

"And I want to—" Kate stopped. Did she dare to tell Erik what she wanted most of all?

"Go on," he said. "I won't laugh."

"I want to—" Kate felt breathless. "When I grow up, I want to marry a really special man. I want to have a home like Mama and Papa have." Even saying the words, Kate felt scared.

But Erik's gaze held hers. "Kate, I want those same things."

As though he, too, were dreaming big dreams, Erik looked out over the creek. A moment later he looked back into her eyes.

"Kate, I want all the things you want. When I'm old enough, I want to marry a Christian—" Erik paused. "A girl just like you."

"Like *me*?" Kate could barely get the words out. Then she remembered. *Oh, no, not like me! If Erik finds out I burned down the barn—*

Kate leaped to her feet. Whirling around, she broke into a run.

"Kate! Stop!" Erik shouted after her.

From behind, Kate heard his great long leaps. As she entered the path through the woods, he caught up.

"Stop!" he called again. "Did I say something wrong?"

"No!" Kate cried. "No, no, no!"

"Then what's wrong?" Erik caught her hand, but Kate broke away and stumbled on.

If I tell Erik what I did, he'll never like me again.

———

By the time the sun set that evening, Kate felt it had been

the longest day she'd ever lived. *I promised to help Ben, but I don't have one idea how to do it. How can I stop Dugan from destroying Jenny's marriage to Ben? I can't even help myself!*

Moving quietly, Kate crept into the bed she shared with Tina.

Kate welcomed the soft bed and the light blanket she pulled up to cover her shoulders. Even more, she felt grateful that she could hide in the darkness. So exhausted that she could barely move, she fell asleep at once.

Sometime during the night she woke up. At first the fire in the barn seemed like a nightmare. Then Kate began shaking. As though the pigs were still squealing, she heard them. As if the roof were falling in, she saw the horses being led from the barn.

Kate's arms moved restlessly. Once more she was passing buckets. But now the pain and terror went much deeper.

Where's Windsong? Kate asked herself again and again. *Is she really dead?* Kate refused to believe that was true.

Again she faced a terrible guilt. *I set the barn on fire.*

With the memory came more pain. Kate's thoughts went round and round. *I can't tell anyone. My family will hate me. Erik will never like me again. I don't even like myself!*

For a long time Kate lay there, staring up at the ceiling she could not see. Gradually the darkness of night faded and light crept into her room.

Through the open windows Kate heard the kitchen door open and close. Careful not to wake Tina, Kate slipped from bed and leaned out.

It was Papa leaving the house, Papa carrying the big family Bible. As Kate watched, he entered the trail that led to Spirit Lake School. Where was he going?

With quick movements Kate pulled on her dress and slipped out of the room. Avoiding the boards that squeaked, she crept down the stairs. Once outside, she started running on the grass next to the trail so that Papa would not hear. Why would he bring his Bible here?

Before long, Kate saw Papa ahead of her. Staying back,

she followed just close enough not to lose sight of him.

Beyond the spring, the trail passed through the woods close to Rice Lake. Soon Papa turned onto a footpath leading up a steep hill. The high point of land overlooked the lake.

When Papa disappeared beyond the rise, Kate walked farther, then crept up the back side of the hill. As she reached the crest, she found herself behind Papa. He sat on the trunk of a fallen tree with the open Bible across his knees.

Early morning fog rose above the still water of Rice Lake. The first rays of sun covered everything with a soft light. Then Papa started turning the pages of his big Bible. Was he trying to get God's help?

As her stepfather read, his head bent over the pages. His shoulders were slumped, the way they had been since the fire.

I lost a horse. Kate swallowed against the pain. *But Papa lost the barn—the shelter he needs for the animals. The hay he needs to feed the cows and horses. Somehow he has to feed us, too.*

Then Papa's head lifted and his shoulders straightened. Kate could almost hear him breathe a sigh of relief. Whatever had happened, she knew her stepfather was all right now.

Suddenly he turned and saw her. Kate jumped, ashamed to be caught watching.

But Papa said, "Come here, Kate," as though not surprised at all. "There's something I want you to see."

Slowly Kate climbed the rest of the way up the hill. Reaching Papa, she sat down next to him on the trunk of the fallen tree. From there the hill dropped straight down ten or fifteen feet to the edge of Rice Lake.

For a few minutes Papa was silent. Kate waited, wondering if he wanted her to notice the still water.

Instead, he looked at his big Bible. "I found a special verse in Psalm 103. 'For as the heavens are high above the earth, so great is his lovingkindness toward them that fear him.' "

"*Fear* Him?" Kate asked. It was easy to fear God after burning down a barn. "He's kind to those who are *afraid* of Him?"

Papa shook his head. "It means those who love and respect Him."

Kate loved and respected God, all right. Yet her thoughts cried out. *How can He possibly love me the way I am? I'm not worth being loved!*

Kate's lips quivered. She pressed them together, trying not to cry. "That's God's love for other people," she said when she could speak. "But it's not for me."

"Because of Windsong?" Papa asked. "Because she died?"

That was part of it, Kate knew, but there was more. *It was my fault!* she wanted to tell him. *I burned down the barn! I killed my own horse!*

But she couldn't say the words. Like a knife turning inside, her shame grew.

"I keep thinking that somehow I should have been able to find Windsong," Papa said, gazing out over the lake. "But when that timber fell—"

"I know, Papa. I'm glad you didn't get hurt worse."

"I couldn't stay. I would have been killed."

"I know," Kate said again. "Thank you for trying." Though she ached with grief, Kate knew Papa had done everything he could.

"I wanted you to have fun with Windsong," Papa went on. "I wanted her to be a special part of your life."

"She is, Papa, she is," Kate answered softly. In that moment she knew. Deep inside, she still was unwilling to believe that Windsong was gone. Until now Kate had never had an animal of her own. How could Windsong be dead?

Papa looked at her and said quietly, "There's still Breeza, Kate."

"But it's not the same," she answered, looking away.

"I know."

"You do?" Kate asked.

Papa nodded. "I lost my first horse."

Kate straightened, suddenly alert, and Papa went on.

"We had a pond in our pasture. She broke through the ice. No one was around, and she couldn't get out."

Kate stared at him, filled with how terrible that was. "Did you hate God?" she asked.

"At first. Finally I understood He wasn't trying to be mean. Sometimes things happen that are just part of life."

"But God could have kept it from happening."

"Yes," Papa said. "He could have. Instead, I learned something."

Kate waited, afraid to speak.

"I learned that no matter what happens to me, God loves me."

Papa waited until Kate's gaze met his. As she saw the kindness in his face, her lips quivered again.

"Maybe this is your time to find that out," Papa said gently.

Kate shook her head, but Papa went on.

"See the earth?" he asked. "The horizon way on the other side of the lake?"

From where she sat high above the water Kate stared across Rice Lake to the distant hills.

"Now, look up to the sky," Papa told her.

Kate's gaze traveled upward to the bluest sky she had ever seen. "All that space between the earth and the sky?" she asked. Again Kate found it difficult to believe. "God really loves me that much?"

Papa nodded. "And He loves you just the way you are."

"Oh, no," Kate answered. "God couldn't possibly love me the way I am."

Again she longed to tell Papa about the barn. *It's my fault that Windsong is gone. Not yours.*

Instead, Kate pushed the thought aside. *If Papa knows the real truth, he'll never love me again.*

A minute longer Papa waited. Then he stood up.

"Papa," Kate asked as they started back to the farm-house. "What if things don't go right? Do you *really* believe God loves you, even though your barn burned down?"

"I *choose* to believe that God loves me," he said quietly. "I believe God loves me because the Bible says so. That means believing He loves me in spite of how I feel—in spite of the bad things that happen to me."

Papa stopped in the middle of the trail. "But there are worse things than having my barn burn down."

This time Kate knew what he was talking about. *It's worse being the one who started the fire!*

18

New Clues

*A*s Papa walked on, Kate argued with herself. *I can be like Papa,* she thought. *Even though everything has gone wrong, I can choose to believe that God loves me.*

Yet fear overwhelmed Kate—fear of what Papa would think.

Her stepfather walked with straight shoulders now. As she watched him, the truth struck Kate. *I will never believe that God loves me unless I tell Papa what I did.*

Kate drew a deep breath. "I have something to tell you."

"Something serious, no doubt," Papa answered, "judging by the look of things."

"Something serious." As they reached the spring, Kate dropped onto the square timbers that held in the water.

"Then maybe you better start," Papa said. The cart for hauling milk cans was nearby, and he sat down.

In spite of Kate's best effort to stay calm, tears welled up in her eyes. "When you hear what I've done, you won't want me to stay in your house!"

"Of course, I want you to stay here. This is your home!"

"But you don't know the worst about me." Tears spilled over, running down Kate's cheeks.

"Yah?" Papa asked. "Then just tell me, Kate."

"It's not your fault that Windsong is gone." Kate's voice was low and ashamed. "I was the one who set your barn on fire."

Papa stared at her. "Why do you think that?"

Now that she had begun, Kate's words tumbled out. When she finished, Papa sat for three or four minutes without speaking.

As though thinking things through, he looked across Rice Lake. His gaze followed an eagle circling above the distant shore. Then at last he looked back at Kate.

"When I met your mama, you were part of the package," he said. "I knew that before I asked your mother to marry me. I wanted you to become my special daughter. I've grown to love you, Kate—love you very much."

Papa paused as if wanting to be sure that she understood. "That love doesn't stop when you do something wrong."

"It doesn't?" Kate felt weak just hearing his words. "Not every father would feel that way."

"No," Papa answered. "Not every father would. But I *do* feel that way. Can you believe me?"

Only an hour before, Kate wouldn't have accepted his words. Now there was something she knew. "Your love is like God's love," she said softly.

"Well, not quite that big!" Papa's grin reminded Kate of Anders, but her giggle ended in tears.

Papa stood up. "If I show you something, will you promise to believe that no matter what you do, I love you?"

Slowly Kate nodded.

Again Papa grinned. "But you don't have to test it out by doing all kinds of wrong things!"

As he started up the steep hill, Kate followed. Halfway

to the farmhouse, they met Anders.

"Kate thinks she burned down the barn," Papa told him.

"You do?" Anders asked Kate.

Dreading what he'd say, she told him what had happened.

"But the fire started at the other end," Anders said. "Papa said it was arson."

"Arson?" Kate asked, unable to believe that it wasn't her fault.

"C'mon," Anders said. "I'll show you."

Anders led Kate to the east end of the barn, the end where Kate had first seen the fire. Only a few charred logs remained. Everything else had fallen in.

"Remember how this looked when we first came out?" Anders asked. "The logs were burning way too fast. Someone threw kerosene against that wall."

"I found kerosene on the ground," Papa explained. "When we started looking, Anders found an empty kerosene can."

At the west end of the barn—the end where the horses had been stabled, Anders showed Kate what Papa had known all along.

The long overhead pole in the center was still in place. The two poles along the sides were also there, giving support to the charred walls. Yet on the other end all three of the poles had fallen.

"If the fire had started here, this would all be gone," Anders said as he pointed to the long center pole. From a nail on that center pole hung a blackened farm lantern.

Kate stared at the lantern, then at Anders. Only a short time before, he and Papa had agreed in saying no to the stallion Kate wanted. Now they were agreeing again. But this time it was to tell her she wasn't to blame.

Kate felt as though a giant weight had fallen off her back. "Thank you," she whispered. Never had she appreciated her brother more.

———————

That afternoon Papa, Anders, and Grandpa took rakes and shovels and started toward the barn. Kate stayed away, not wanting to watch what they were doing.

When they had searched the ruins, they came to her. It was Papa who said, "Kate, there's no sign that Windsong was in the barn."

Kate felt weak with relief. "You mean—" She had to hear it again.

"Windsong wasn't inside the barn when it burned."

"She really didn't die in the fire? I can't believe it!" Kate felt like doing cartwheels across the lawn, like leaping in the air. Yet tears rolled down her cheeks.

Then Kate realized she had another problem. "If Windsong wasn't in the barn, where *is* she?"

"That's what we don't know," Papa answered. "I doubt that she got away by herself."

Kate doubted it too. After Windsong's escape, Kate had been careful to slip a wire in place, securing the latch.

"We think someone stole her," Anders told Kate. "Maybe he set the fire to hide what he did. Maybe he burned the barn in revenge."

"So it's Dugan?" Kate asked.

"We think so," Papa told her.

When Erik came over that evening, Kate explained about the forgotten lantern.

"Why didn't you tell me?" Erik asked when he heard the story. "What's a friend for if I can't help when something's wrong?"

Kate hung her head. She was finding out about Erik too.

When the family talked about what to do, they decided they were back to the same thing. If they could find Windsong, she would lead them to Dugan.

"But how can we find Windsong?" Kate asked. "The

night of the fire it rained hard. Wouldn't every trace of a horse be washed out?"

They started by searching the trail that led to the main road. So many wagons had passed through that it was impossible to know if Windsong had gone that way. From there Kate, Anders, Lars, and Erik divided up the farm and spread out, each one taking a different direction. Not one of them found anything.

The next morning Papa hitched up Dolly and Florie. He and Grandpa put a tent, food, and scythes in the back of the farm wagon. A man had given Papa permission to cut wild hay on his land south of Grantsburg. For now they would cut and stack the hay in the meadows. Later on, when it was dry, they would bring it home.

Before Papa left, he talked to Anders.

"I don't want to leave, but I don't have any choice," Papa said. "We have to have hay for winter. For Kate's sake, keep looking for Windsong."

Then Papa turned to Kate. "I'm proud of you," he said.

"Proud of *me*?" The idea shocked Kate. It was just what she wanted—having the family proud of her. But after all this? "How can you be proud of *me*? I could have burned down your barn!"

"Twice now," Papa said, looking Kate straight in the eyes. "Twice now you've told me the truth, even though it was very hard."

———

Early the next morning, Kate woke up while it was still dark. For a time she lay quietly, thinking about Windsong. *What happened to her? Where is she now?*

Countless times Kate had asked herself those questions. Now she had an even bigger one. Does God really love *me*?

Kate had no doubt that God loved *everyone* enough to send His Son to earth. Kate knew and believed that Jesus had died on the cross. When she told Him she was sorry for her sins, His death became real to her—and so did God's forgiveness.

But here was something else. *Does God love me, even when everything goes wrong?* Kate wondered.

As if she and Papa were still sitting near Rice Lake, Kate remembered looking from the earth to the sky. *As high as the heavens are above the earth.*

She couldn't begin to imagine how much space there was between the earth and the sky. *So great is His love for those who love and respect Him.*

Maybe that love is like Papa's love, Kate thought. Though she left a lantern in the barn, Papa still cared about her. But what if she hadn't had a stepfather like him? Would she ever understand God's love?

Quietly Kate crept out of bed. Without making a sound, she tiptoed to the windows. From her second-floor room, she looked across Rice Lake.

Seeing the still water, Kate remembered her question to Papa. "What if things don't go right?"

"Then I choose to believe God loves me because the Bible says so," Papa had told her. "That means believing God loves me, in spite of how I feel—in spite of the bad things that happen to me."

Maybe that's what all of us have to do, Kate decided. *Whether we have a good father or one who doesn't care.*

In this last week of August the days were still warm, but the nights cool. Early morning fog hung above the water.

What will the day bring? Kate wondered. *Maybe I'll find Windsong!*

Then fear grabbed her thoughts. *Maybe I won't!*

Suddenly Kate felt sure of something. *I'll have to make my choice. Do I believe God really loves* me?

As the sunlight grew stronger, Kate flipped her braid over her shoulder. With her eyes wide open, she prayed.

*You promised that you love me, God. No matter what happens
with Windsong, I choose to believe that you do!*

———————

Later that morning Mama held up the blue dress, fitting
it to Kate. When Mama was ready to pin up the hem, she
measured carefully.

"You've grown a whole inch since your last dress!"

"I have?" Kate asked in surprise. Always it was Anders
who measured higher and higher on the doorpost.

That afternoon Kate and Mama were still in the kitchen
when Anders burst in. "There's a letter for you, Kate. You
better see what it is."

Kate glanced down at the postmark. Strange! It was
blurred so she couldn't tell where the letter came from. But
stranger still was the envelope. It was made from the most
expensive paper Kate had ever seen. Yet it had no return
address.

"Who would send me something like this?"

Inside, the single sheet of paper was folded in half. Un-
like the envelope, the stationery was ordinary writing paper.

When Kate read the typed message, her hands started
to shake. "I hate it! I hate it!" She threw the page down on
the table.

Mama hurried over. "What's wrong, Kate?"

"It's so horrible I don't want to touch it!"

When Anders read the words aloud, they seemed even
more frightening.

```
Just w it.
I'll get even with  ll of you.
```

"The letter *a* is missing," Anders said.

Mama looked angry. "It's only a coward who sends a
letter without signing it!"

"A coward!" Kate exclaimed. "Whoever wrote this let-

ter has already gotten even! It must be the man who set
fire to the barn!"

"And Ben's house and Charlie's hay wagon," Anders
said. "It has to be Dugan! But where is he?"

Just thinking about the kind of person who would do
such terrible things frightened Kate.

Mama's usually peaceful face looked troubled. "I wish
Papa was home," she said. Yet all of them knew he
wouldn't be back for at least two days.

"What awful thing will Dugan do next?" Kate asked.
"If he set a fire three times, will he try again?"

Not even Mama had any idea, but Anders was sure of
one thing. "Whatever Dugan thinks up, it'll be dangerous."

Kate stared at him. "Anders, you do not make me feel
good at all!"

"I don't think I should. We better be mighty careful."

"You mean—"

"If someone's mind is sick, who can tell what he'll do?"

Kate trembled. Once more she looked down at the message. As she read the words again, she thought of something. "I've seen typing like this before."

Kate jumped up and ran from the room. When she returned, she laid Ben's letter next to the other one. "Look!"
she said.

```
De r K te,

I  m in big trouble.  If Dug n wins,
no job, no wedding, no Jenny.  Ple se
 sk f mily to pr y for me.

                    Ben
```

"When I read Ben's letter, I thought he didn't know
how to spell all the words," Kate said. "But it's the typewriter. The letter *a* is missing!"

"Ah-ha!" Anders exclaimed. "And the letters are written on the same typewriter! Probably a typewriter at Nevers Dam."

"Let's go!" Kate exclaimed. "If Dugan is there again, we have to warn Ben!"

"And put a stop to all this!" Anders growled.

By the time he returned with Erik, Kate was ready to leave. Erik swung up on Breeza. Riding bareback on Wildfire, Anders reached down a hand and helped Kate up behind him.

"Be careful," Mama told them as they said goodbye. "If that man wants revenge, he must be filled with hate."

19

Nevers Dam

"We need to hurry," Kate said to Erik as they left the farm. "We have to find Dugan before he hurts Ben again."

As Kate and the boys turned south on the road to Trade Lake, Lutfisk caught up with them.

"Go on home!" Anders commanded.

With his head hanging low, the dog started back. A short distance off, he sat down. With his sad brown gaze on Anders, he wagged his tail.

Anders called to him. "You're lonesome, aren't you?"

Lutfisk tipped his head to one side and yipped.

"You think I'm spending too much time with the horses?"

As though he understood, Lutfisk yipped again.

"All right! C'mon, boy!" Anders commanded. "I haven't forgotten you!"

Like a child let out of school, Lutfisk leaped up and raced to Anders. As the horses set out again, the dog walked or ran along next to Wildfire.

"From what Papa said, Dugan might have it in for anyone who does the right thing," Kate told the boys.

"If that man is crazy enough to set buildings on fire, there's nothing he won't try," Anders said.

Reaching forward, Erik patted the chestnut's neck. "Why didn't Dugan take Breeza too?"

"I betcha that's what he planned." As he rode along, directly in front of Kate, Anders shrugged. "Lutfisk jumped through the screen because he knew something was going on. I think Dugan had already set the fire. When Lutfisk went after him, Dugan grabbed Windsong and took off."

Anders had never given up the idea that Dugan sold his horses, then stole them back to sell them again and again.

Kate's fists clenched just thinking about the kind of person who would set three fires. "I want to find Dugan," she said. "But I dread seeing him again."

"I don't want to meet him on a dark night," Erik answered.

Kate sighed. "We might *have* to meet him on a dark night!"

Twisting around, Anders grinned at Kate. "Be careful, my little sister," he warned with a low and mysterious voice. "Wherever you go, Dugan will follow. Without making a sound, he'll creep about on his little cat feet."

"Stop it, Anders!" Kate exclaimed.

"He'll sneak up on you!"

Kate slapped his back. Already she'd had the same thoughts. Anders didn't need to add to them. Instead, Kate wished she could forget Mama's words. *If that man wants revenge, he must be full of hate.*

The eighteen-mile ride to Nevers Dam seemed to last forever. When Anders and Erik stopped the horses at Cushing, Lutfisk flopped down beside them to rest.

By late afternoon Kate and the boys passed through the village of Wolf Creek. As they followed the dirt road south, Kate caught a view of the river. From shore to shore it was filled with logs. Kate remembered what Ben had said.

All through August the gatekeeper at Nevers was not

allowed to open the dam. During that month, steamboats at Taylors Falls and farther downstream used the St. Croix whenever they liked to bring in passengers and supplies.

"When the dam is closed, the river builds up for twelve to fourteen miles," Anders told Kate. "Logging camps roll their logs into the water. When the sawmills at Stillwater want more logs, they send a message to Nevers. The gate-keeper lets the logs through."

"What about the boats downstream?" Kate asked. "What if someone opened the dam at the wrong time?"

"No one will," Anders said. "It would give the dam a really bad name."

"But what if someone did? All those logs would crash into them."

"Don't worry your head about it," Anders told her. "The men at Nevers warn the steamboat captains. They have plenty of time to get out of the way."

Just the same, Kate couldn't help thinking about the danger. She had always wanted to ride on a paddlewheeler. Yet she wouldn't like to be on board with a mighty rush of logs coming at her. They could ram right through the hull of a boat.

A cluster of buildings told them they had reached Nevers Dam. Set back from the steep riverbank, one building looked like a bunkhouse, another like a cookhouse. Stables were nearby, too, as well as a long shed and a farmhouse.

Ben was alone in the office, entering figures in a large book. As they walked in the door, he jumped up. "You're just in time!"

When Kate asked how he was doing, Ben had good news. "Today Mr. Frawley said, 'Ben, if all goes well, I'll keep training you for the office.'"

Ben shook his head. "But if one more thing goes wrong—" A worried look crept into his eyes. "If I do any-thing that hurts the good name of Nevers Dam—"

"You're fired?" Anders asked.

"No job. No wedding. No Jenny."

As Kate described the threatening letter they'd received, Ben's face flushed with anger.

"We think Dugan is somewhere around here," Kate said. She showed him the note, and Ben agreed that it was written on the office typewriter.

"Dugan must be sneaking in at night," Ben said. "But I can't figure out where he comes from. I watch the woods. I watch the road—"

He broke off. "Tomorrow is an extra big payday. Besides all the usual workers, we'll pay off the men who have been repairing the dam. If Dugan knows about that, he'll steal the money tonight."

"Do you lock the office?" Kate asked, knowing that most people in the area left their doors unlocked.

"Yah, sure," Ben answered. "But I think Dugan has a key of his own. That's why it looks like I take the money. There's never a sign of a break-in."

"Is Mr. Frawley here now?" Erik asked.

"You just missed him," Ben said. "He moved to St. Croix Falls a couple years ago when his son Russ started school."

Ben grinned. "That's why he needs *me* to keep an eye on things!"

Ben's grin faded. "Usually Mr. Frawley rides a horse back and forth, but tomorrow he'll row up the river. He'll bring a gear the men need to finish repairs on the dam."

"Wouldn't it be easier to take it by wagon?" Erik asked.

Ben shook his head. "Not with the road we've got. It's okay for riding a horse, but the gear is too big for that."

Ben started for the door. "Let's go eat. Then let's wait here in the dark for Dugan. If we don't catch him this time—" He hurried out of the office.

Anders and the others wasted no time in following. The cook had a good meal ready, both for the men who worked at the dam and for those who farmed the land connected with Nevers. The cook had no problem stretching the food for three more.

When all of them had finished eating, Ben offered to

show Kate and the boys the dam. As they started to leave, Kate noticed a painting near the door. In front of a steamboat stood a girl with deep brown eyes. Her smile leaped off the canvas.

Kate felt drawn to her, as if the girl were someone she'd like to know. "Who is she?" Kate asked Ben.

"Libby? Mr. Frawley says she was a captain's daughter. She traveled up and down the river with her pa. When they came to Taylors Falls, a traveling artist asked if he could paint her."

Anders looked over Kate's shoulder. "Who's that boy? He looks about my age."

Ben grinned. "He lived on the steamboat too. Sometime I'll tell you a story about him."

Kate gazed at the boat's large paddles. "What would it be like living on a riverboat?" she asked.

"You'd be curious every minute," Anders told her. "It was a dangerous life!"

"Lots of snags," Ben said. "All kinds of logs ready to bust a hole in your boat. Ice in the spring and fall—"

"And now and then a shady character came aboard." Erik's eyes gleamed with fun. "You'd like that, Kate."

"You'd like the cardsharps and thieves," her brother teased. "There'd always be something exciting happening."

"Exciting, all right!" Ben said. "Those old steamboats weren't the safest. Sometimes they blew up!"

"But think about it!" Kate said. "Think of all the places Libby saw, all the people she met."

Erik grinned. "All the adventures she had! And the mysteries she solved!"

Again Kate wished she could have known Libby. Kate felt sure they would have been best friends.

Outside, Ben led them toward the river. A wagon road passed down the hill onto a large earthen dike. When they came within sight of Nevers Dam, Kate gasped.

Her surprise pleased Ben. "You like it?" he asked.

Though he had described the size to her, Kate hadn't begun to grasp how long six hundred and twenty-four feet could be.

"It's the biggest pile-driven dam in the world," Ben told her proudly.

Huge log timbers had been set in boxlike "cribs" and filled with wagonloads of rock. These piers provided the foundation and support for the fifteen gates that were raised or lowered to control the flow of water.

Above the dam, a wagon bridge linked Wisconsin to Minnesota. As Kate and the boys followed Ben onto the bridge, they passed over the gates of the dam. On the other side of the river, they came to an even longer dike leading to the Minnesota shore.

When they walked back toward Wisconsin, Ben stopped on the section of bridge built above the largest gate. From where they stood, Kate had a good view of the large lake created by the dam and the dikes. As far upstream as she could see, the lake held logs, ready to be sent through the dam.

"What if someone fell in?" Kate asked Ben. "With all those logs no one would find him."

"Just don't fall in," Ben said simply.

Leaning against the railing, Kate stared down. Only a small amount of water passed through the gate. "Is this the big bear trap you told me about?" she asked.

Again Ben looked proud. "It's the largest gate in the world." He explained how it worked.

Eighty feet wide and twenty feet high, the bear trap, or Lang gate, was named after Robert Lang, the construction supervisor who designed it. Like an upside down V, it was hinged at the top.

When open, the gate lay flat on the bed of the river, allowing any size log, even thirty-six-foot logs floating sideways, to pass through. When shut, the gate held back the water, creating the pond that extended twelve or fourteen miles upstream.

Nearby were the gears and long cables that controlled

the gate. By using a lever or wheel, even a boy or girl could open or close the eighty-foot gate.

"Two more days, and we open her up," Ben said. "When that happens, you should see the rush of logs!" For the entire month of August, logs had collected in the lakelike area, ready to be sent to sawmills in Stillwater.

When the sun slipped behind the trees on the Minnesota bluff, Kate felt the coolness of the water. As she pulled on her sweater, she noticed a break in the trees where the bluff looked bare.

"They took rocks and gravel from there to build the dikes," Ben explained. But he was growing restless now, and Kate knew he was anxious to return to the office.

As Anders and Ben went ahead, Kate and Erik lagged behind.

"There's something that's been bothering me," Erik told Kate as they stood on the section of bridge above the bear trap. "Why didn't you tell me when you thought you burned down the barn?"

Startled, Kate met his gaze. "I was afraid," she answered. "I knew you were already disappointed in me."

"Disappointed?" Erik asked. "What do you mean?"

"That day in Charlie's stable."

Erik had forgotten about it. "Sure, I was disappointed," he admitted. "But all of us have times when we say things we shouldn't. Do you think *I'm* perfect?"

Kate stared at him, afraid to answer.

"Do you?" Erik asked.

"Well—almost."

Erik grinned. "But not quite. What if *I* had burned down the barn?"

"You'd never do such a thing!"

"But what if I did? What if I accidentally set fire to it? Would you tell me you didn't want me for a friend?"

That wasn't difficult. Kate shook her head.

"Why are you trying so hard to be perfect?" Erik asked softly. "I believe in you, Kate. Just be the way you are."

Kate's throat tightened. Unable to speak, she looked up at him. She wished she could tell Erik how much his friendship meant to her.

When his gaze met hers, Erik caught her hand and squeezed it.

"C'mon," he said. "We better get up to the office. If Ben needs help, we can't hear him this far away."

"You go ahead," Kate said. "I'll be up in a minute."

When Erik reached the curve in the dike, he turned and waved. Kate waved back, then watched until Erik was out of sight.

Mama's right, Kate thought as she looked down at the river. *This is my growing-up year.* Sometimes it made her afraid, but right now Kate was spilling over with dreams. For the rest of her life, Erik would be the person she used to measure any other boy she met.

On the Minnesota bluff the trees looked black against the orange sky. For a moment longer Kate stood there, enjoying the beauty of the sunset. Usually she liked being in on the excitement of whatever happened. Tonight was different. She didn't want to sit in a stuffy room, waiting for Dugan. She wanted to think about Erik.

Then Lutfisk raced down the dike from the Wisconsin shore. When he reached Kate, she knelt on the bridge and scratched him behind the ears. "Good boy!" she told him. "Good dog!"

Wagging his tail, Lutfisk yipped with pleasure. All at once he squirmed away. Standing with his ears and body alert, his gaze followed the wagon road across the top of the dam.

"What is it, boy?" Kate asked. "What do you hear?"

In the next instant Lutfisk lit out for the Minnesota side of the river. Soon he stopped and looked back. Turning toward Kate, he woofed, as though trying to get her to follow.

When Kate took only a few steps, Lutfisk raced on. Clearly, something was bothering him, or he wouldn't be so excited. Yet Kate felt uneasy. She wished Anders or Erik were here—that she didn't have to follow the dog by her-self. What if Dugan was around and she didn't know it?

Still on the section of bridge over the bear trap, Kate stopped. Lutfisk ran back to her. Within a few feet of Kate, he planted himself squarely in front of her and barked.

"What do you want, Lutfisk?" Kate asked. Whatever was bothering the dog, it was important.

In answer, he once more ran a short distance, then stopped. Looking back toward Kate, he woofed a quick, ex-cited bark.

By now Kate's curiosity was stronger than her uneasi-ness. Quickly she pulled off her sweater and tied it around the bridge railing. If Anders or Erik saw the sweater, they would know where she had gone.

Then Kate hurried as fast as she could after Lutfisk.

20

Out of the Darkness

The dog stayed on the wagon road as it passed onto the dike for the Minnesota side. Near the bottom of the bluff, Lutfisk left the road and disappeared into the trees.

As Kate reached the trees, she peered into the growing dusk. A short distance off the path was an outline blacker than the gray light. A horse lifted its head and whinnied. Windsong!

Kate broke into a run. Reaching Windsong, she flung her arms around the mare's neck. Sobbing, Kate buried her face in the mare's mane. "Windsong! Windsong! I can't believe it's you!"

For only a moment Kate stood there. With tears streaming down her cheeks, she untied the lead rope and swung into the saddle. Feeling a desperate need to hurry, Kate turned Windsong onto the road back to the Wisconsin shore.

Lutfisk ran alongside, yipped, then raced ahead. Near the beginning of the dike, the dog stopped. From deep in his throat he growled.

As Windsong caught up, a man stepped out from behind a large tree. Before Kate could get out of his way, he grabbed the bridle. Jerking back in surprise, Kate almost fell out of the saddle.

Her heart lurched as she saw the man from the blacksmith shop. It had to be Dugan. His handsome face looked hard and mean with hate.

"I thought I heard you coming!" he cried.

Frantically Kate kicked her heels against Windsong's sides. "Go on, girl!"

But Dugan clung to the bridle. "This time you're not getting away!"

Filled with panic, Kate glanced around, searching for a way of escape. Even if Anders or Erik came down to the bridge, they wouldn't see her. In the fading light she was too far away.

"Let me go!" Kate yelled. "Frawley will catch you when he comes!"

Dugan's eyes lit up. "He's coming up the river?"

Kate gasped. She had told Dugan just what he wanted to know.

"When?" Dugan demanded.

Kate shrugged, trying to pretend it wasn't important. But her thoughts leaped ahead. What would Dugan's twisted mind think up next?

He glared up at her. "When is Frawley coming?" Dugan's cruel voice threatened Kate. "I asked you a question. Answer me!"

In that instant Lutfisk became a snarling monster. As he leaped at Dugan, Kate saw her chance. In one swift movement she dropped down on the other side of the horse. But Dugan stood between her and the dike. She had no choice but to go in the opposite direction.

Desperate with fear, Kate turned toward the Minnesota bluff. As she raced across the uneven ground, she stumbled, caught herself and hurried on.

When she slipped beneath the cover of trees, the dusk deepened. For several more steps Kate staggered on. Then her eyes grew used to the fading light.

From behind, she heard a yip, then a yowl of pain. Kate turned, unwilling to leave Lutfisk behind. As she started back, she heard a snarl. The dog was holding his own, giving her the time she needed to escape. Once again Kate fled through the dusk.

The hill was rising now, the bluff growing steep beneath her feet. Before long, Kate's side ached from running. Finally she had no choice but to slow down to a fast walk. As the trees thinned out, it was easier to see.

Ahead lay a long, barren stretch of ground—the slash in the hillside where builders had taken gravel. Bushes and small trees dotted the ground.

When Kate paused, wondering where to go, she heard noises from behind. Someone crashing through the brush. Dugan!

As though in a nightmare, Kate searched for cover. The bushes ahead offered little protection. Even if she crouched down, Dugan would find her.

Having no other choice, Kate started running again. Soon her breath came in great ragged gasps.

Once she turned around. No one in sight yet. If only she could find a hiding place!

By the sound she knew when Dugan reached the gravel. He was gaining on her! With her last bit of strength Kate stumbled on.

Then she saw it. A small shed, off to one side of the open area, partly hidden by a scrubby tree. It seemed too good to be true. Yet if she hid inside, Dugan might run past, not seeing her.

Reaching the shed, Kate raised the strong wooden bar that held the door shut. As she opened the door, it creaked. Quickly Kate slipped inside and pulled the door shut behind her.

Standing there in the dark, she drew in great gasps of air. She couldn't have kept on another minute, and she knew it.

Moments later, Kate heard heavy footsteps, running on gravel. Without moving a muscle, she waited. When the steps passed beyond the shed, she breathed a sigh of relief.

Around Kate, the shed was pitch black, but it didn't matter. Dugan had gone on. She was safe!

Kate's shoulders heaved as she again breathed deeply. But then from somewhere nearby, she heard footsteps. Stealthy footsteps moving closer and closer.

Suddenly a voice thundered out. "I know you're in there!"

Startled, Kate jumped. As she jerked back, she fell against metal. Cold and hard, it clattered into something else.

Filled with agony, Kate waited. If Dugan were bluffing, pretending that he knew where she was, there was no hiding now. What would that terrible man do?

Kate felt for the door, ready to push it open, ready to run for her life. Could she somehow get past Dugan?

Then Kate heard his voice.

"You think I don't take care of my horses?"

Kate's stomach flip-flopped. He still remembered that? With dread she recalled Mama's words. *If that man wants revenge, he must be filled with hate.* Dugan was filled with hate, all right.

"I'll show you how I take care of things!" he shouted.

In the next moment Kate heard the wooden bar drop in place. She was locked in!

In spite of her fear of Dugan, Kate pounded against the door. "Let me out!"

Dugan laughed, a laugh from deep in his throat. "You're staying here. I've got a job to do!"

"A job?" Kate trembled. If only she could keep him talking, maybe help would come. "What job?"

"At the dam. I'll get even with Frawley for firing me! I'll get even with that uncle of yours!"

"You won't get even with anyone!" Kate shouted. Again she pounded on the door. "Let me out!"

But Dugan only laughed. Kate hated the evil sound.

"You'll see," he told her. "I'll get the payroll and Frawley, too. I'll get him when he comes up the river."

A cold fist tightened around Kate's heart. She hated herself for giving things away. What if Frawley lost his life because of her?

"You won't get the money!" Kate stormed. "You won't get *anyone!*"

"That's what you think!" Dugan's voice was cold and hard. "I get even with *everyone* who tries to stop me. That includes you and your brother! And that boyfriend of yours!"

Kate gulped. How much did Dugan know about her? Her stomach tightened with panic as she thought what he could do.

I'll get out, Kate promised herself. *I'll warn them if it's the last thing I do!*

But something was terribly wrong. Not even Lutfisk had been able to follow her. What had happened to the dog?

Again Kate pounded against the door. Dugan's voice stopped her.

"I don't care if you *ever* get out! You can yell all you want. No one will hear you!"

Then silence filled the night. A silence even more dreadful than Dugan's cruel voice.

Where is he? Kate thought. Whirling around, she stared into the darkness. Was there another door to the shed?

Even her knees trembled. *What if he's sneaking up on me? What if he's here in the darkness, and I don't know it?*

So afraid that she could barely breathe, Kate waited, listening. After some time, she felt sure that Dugan had to be gone. Even now he must be crossing the bridge, creeping up on the office. Even now he could be looking in the window, planning his worst.

What was happening to Anders and Erik? To Ben? What were they doing? Filled with the terror of it, Kate swallowed hard.

If they left the office to search for her, Dugan would creep in and steal the money. But how could they *not* look? All of them would wonder where she was.

I've got to warn them, Kate told herself again. *There has to be a way out of this awful place!*

Her hands spread in front of her, Kate felt the wooden wall. Across the boards she moved her hands until she found the crack for the door. Making sure she did not lose that door, she turned slowly, forcing herself to take a quarter turn at a time.

Whichever way she looked, Kate could not see even a hint of dusk. No moon or starlight shone through a window. Not even a crack of light gave the hope of an opening.

With her hands against the wall to guide her, Kate started around the shed. Before long, she fell over something—something big and heavy. No doubt the shed was used for storing equipment when the dam was built.

Picking herself up, Kate drew a deep breath and tried to calm herself. Once more, she found the wall. Carefully she felt every inch, as high as she could reach.

In a corner she came against objects leaning every which way. One of them clattered to the ground. Bending down, Kate felt along the length of it. A wooden handle, she was sure. A curved bar, sharpened at both ends. A pick for breaking up rock! Maybe she could break out of the shed!

Filled with hope, Kate dragged the pick to the nearest wall. There she discovered she could not lift the heavy tool, let alone swing it against the wood.

Pushing aside her disappointment, Kate kept on around the shed, feeling every crack in the wall. When she completed the circle, she had to face the truth. There was only one door, and it was barred shut by a strong piece of wood.

Once more, Kate pounded against the door. Overcome by panic, she beat her fists against the wood until her hands were scraped and bleeding.

No answer came.

Again and again, Kate rammed her body against the door. Not once did it move. Not even an inch.

Finally Kate had to give up. Sinking down on the dirt floor, she faced the reality of what had happened. No one knew where she was. How could anyone possibly find her?

As if she could see them, Kate imagined Erik and Anders coming down to the river to look for her. "Where are you, Kate?" they'd call, thinking she was teasing them.

But then, knowing Dugan might be about, they'd get worried. Kate could almost hear them talking. "Where is she?" they'd ask. "What happened to her?" Even her fun-loving brother would be worried.

Well, I did one thing right, Kate thought. *At least I left my sweater on the bridge. They'll know which way to search.*

Will they? The two words whirled around in Kate's mind. *Will they know I crossed the bridge? Or will they think I fell in the river?*

Tears welled up in Kate's eyes as the awful truth struck her. *If they think I've drowned, they'll search the river, not here. They could spend all night looking in the wrong place!*

Kate leaped to her feet. "Anders! Erik! Ben!" she cried. She shouted until her voice was hoarse, but no help came.

Once more Kate sank to the ground. As though she were actually seeing it, she imagined Frawley coming up the river. Dugan opening the dam. The logs sweeping out, crashing into Frawley's boat.

Kate began sobbing. *I have to warn him! Somehow I have to get there in time! But how can I escape?* Filled with desperation, Kate wept until she could cry no more.

When she reached for her handkerchief, she couldn't find it. At first she thought she had pushed it deeper into a pocket. Then she realized it was truly gone.

I can't even keep track of a hankie! Kate thought, and began sobbing again.

At last she drew a long shuddering breath. "It will take a miracle," Kate told herself. "Only a miracle will get me out."

Strangely the word comforted her. It reminded her of God. "Well, why not?"

Only then did Kate realize she had spoken aloud. "Why not?" she asked again, but this time she was talking to God. "If your love is so big it fills all the space between the earth and the sky, why can't you do *another* miracle?"

For the first time since being locked in, Kate felt better. Settling back, she leaned against the wall. As she stretched out her feet, she wondered how many spiders would crawl over her legs. But then Kate started to pray.

"I didn't see the bear, God, but I saw the terrible things he did. I don't see you either, God, but I see the *good* things you do! I *know* you love me. I *know* you are big enough, even for this!"

Kate had no idea how long she had prayed when she saw one tiny sliver of gray light. High on the wall at one end of the shed was a narrow crack in the boards. Every other wall looked as solid as Kate had thought.

In the dim light Kate could barely see the tools and pieces of machinery. Again she got up and searched for a way out. There really was only one opening—the door by which she had come in.

Once more Kate felt the hopelessness of her situation. Where was Dugan by now? Had he stolen the money? What had happened to Anders and Erik and Ben? What had happened to Lutfisk?

Tears welled up in her eyes, but this time Kate brushed them aside. She didn't have time to cry. If she was seeing the first light of dawn, Frawley was coming up the river. Maybe she could still warn him in time.

Sitting on the ground, her back against the wall, Kate tried to work out a plan. Only one prayer came to mind. "Lord, show me what to do."

Just then she heard a noise in the gravel outside. Kate sat without moving. *Is it Dugan?* she wondered. *Has he come back?*

21

Help!

Then Kate heard a quick woof. Lutfisk was outside!

Kate leaped to her feet. "Help!" she cried, pounding on the door. "Help!"

In the next instant she heard the wooden bar go up. Suddenly the door opened.

"Kate!" exclaimed Erik. "It's really you!" As if wondering if he was seeing things, Erik pulled her into the light.

"Erik?" Kate asked. Of course it was Erik, and Lutfisk and Breeza, too. Though Kate couldn't believe it, Erik stood right in front of her.

With one quick movement he opened his arms, and Kate walked into them. As she felt his strong arms around her, Kate started crying again.

When Erik stepped back, she saw the relief in his face. But his eyes were wet with tears.

"Am I glad to see you! Everyone thought you were—" Erik stopped, unable to go on.

"Don't say it!" Kate exclaimed. "Don't even mention the word!" Kneeling down, she hugged Lutfisk too.

"We spent all night combing the river," Erik told her when he could speak again. "Everyone who works at Nevers went up and down the Wisconsin side. All night I kept hoping—"

Erik swallowed hard, as though he had a lump in his throat. "They turned on the lights—the electric lights they used to work on the dam. We all searched the piers next to the dam. We searched the gates, looking for *anything*—

"Lutfisk came up to the office," Erik went on. "That's what was really scary, Kate. He led us back to the bridge. He kept racing from one end of the bridge to the other, and we thought you had fallen in."

Erik's face crumpled, and Kate guessed how awful it had been for him.

"At first light one of the men pulled your sweater out of the river," he said. "It was near the bear trap gate, caught between two logs."

Tears streamed down Erik's face. "Anders sat down on the bridge. He put his head in his hands and cried."

"Anders *cried*?" Kate asked.

"He cried so hard that his shoulders shook."

"And you?" Kate asked. "What happened to you?"

"I thought—" Erik cleared his throat. "I thought I would have known if you died."

"So you kept looking?"

Erik nodded.

"But how did you find me?" Kate asked. "With all these woods, how did you know where to go?"

"I couldn't stand hearing them talk," Erik said. "I took Breeza and went the rest of the way across the river. I wasn't going to give up. Not yet. Not for anything. But without Breeza I wouldn't have found you."

Erik reached inside his shirt, pulled out Kate's hankie and laid it in her hands.

Kate stared at it, then at Erik. "Where did you find it?"

"Near a log at this end of the dike. It was pushed down, almost hidden. I would have missed it. But Breeza picked it up in his teeth. That's when I understood what Lutfisk had been doing—trying to get us to the Minnesota side."

For the first time since finding Kate, Erik grinned. "When I took the hankie from Breeza, he whinnied. Windsong whinnied back."

"So you found her? She's all right?" Kate asked.

"I moved her in case Dugan is still around. I tied her lead rope to a tree down the hill a ways."

Erik sounded as if that were the best news in the world, but Kate disagreed. "That means Dugan is still here."

"He locked you in?"

Kate nodded. "Did Dugan get the payroll?"

"Yup." But Erik sounded as if he hardly cared. "When we were out looking for you."

"Dugan must have dropped my sweater in the water," Kate said. "We better hurry. When Jim Frawley comes up the river, Dugan will open the bear trap."

Erik leaped into Breeza's saddle. Reaching down a hand, he pulled Kate up. As she settled herself behind Erik, Breeza started back.

Partway across the gravel hillside, Kate heard a noise. "Stop!" she whispered as she tugged Erik's shirt.

When Erik reined in, Kate listened. A moment later she heard hoofbeats. Was Dugan coming back?

Kate's fingers knotted into fists. But then Breeza whinnied. From the woods came an answering whinny. Windsong!

Erik urged Breeza on. Before long, Windsong appeared. Her head held to one side to avoid stepping on her lead rope, she cantered across the open area.

When Erik stopped Breeza, Kate slid to the ground. As she threw her arms around Windsong, the mare nuzzled her neck.

A coil of rope was buckled next to the saddle. Seeing it made Kate both curious and uneasy. *I wonder why Dugan has rope along?*

But as Kate leaped into the saddle all her love for Windsong welled up. She was riding her own horse again!

Erik led the way down the rest of the hill. As if glad they were all together again, Lutfisk ran in and out between the horses.

Riding onto the Minnesota dike, Kate peered ahead. To her surprise the bridge was empty. Had the men given up their search?

Erik held up his hand in warning. "It's too quiet. I want to find out what's going on before I bring you into the open. Maybe they've set a trap for Dugan."

As they drew close to the bridge, Erik led Kate down the steep side of the dike. On the downstream side of the dam, he pulled her into the cover of trees. Lutfisk remained close to Windsong.

"Stay here," Erik whispered to Kate. "Breeza's hooves make so much noise I don't want to take him on the bridge."

Erik slid down from the horse. While Kate held Breeza's bridle, Erik climbed back up the side of the dike. Moving quickly and quietly, he hurried onto the wagon road.

For a few minutes Lutfisk waited with Kate and the horses. Then the dog tore after Erik.

Kate grinned. *I've always known dogs are a good judge of character!*

Before long, Erik and Lutfisk crossed the long section of bridge above the bear trap gate. Seconds later Kate heard a quiet movement behind her. Without doubt she knew what it was.

In the next instant she moved her feet ahead, just behind Windsong's front legs. As Dugan reached for Breeza's bridle, Kate pressed her toe against Windsong's left side. The mare's foreleg came up, striking Dugan in the shin.

"Ow! Ow! Ow!" he cried, stumbling back.

Kate squeezed her heels into Windsong's sides, and the mare moved out. As Windsong scrambled up the side of the dike, Dugan ripped Breeza's reins out of Kate's hand. In spite of his pain, Dugan pulled himself into Breeza's saddle.

At the top of the dike Kate turned Windsong toward the

Wisconsin shore. As Kate urged her on, the mare's hooves thundered on the wooden bridge. Breeza was not far behind.

Far ahead, close to the Wisconsin shore, Erik whirled around. Seeing Kate, he broke into a run, racing back to her and Dugan.

A short distance beyond the big bear trap, Kate grew hopeful. Maybe she would get away after all!

But in the next moment something changed. No hoofbeats echoed from behind. Kate wondered why.

Twisting around, she looked back. Near the large gears that operated the bear trap, Dugan had stopped. As he stumbled toward the lever that lowered the mighty gate, Kate's panic changed to terror.

"Even a boy or girl can open the gate," Ben had said. Kate felt sure of one thing. *Dugan is going to do it!*

As Kate reined in, she glanced downstream. Not far away was a man in a small boat. With his back turned toward them, he was rowing up the river.

Was it Frawley? Kate felt sure that it was. *That great rush of logs will be slamming against him!*

Kate dug in her heels. "Go on, Windsong!" she urged the mare. "Go on!"

As Kate raced back to Dugan, the man looked up. His face filled with hate, he reached out for the lever.

"Stop!" Kate cried. "Don't do it!"

With one quick movement, Dugan pulled the lever. In the next instant the gate dropped down. With a mighty whoosh the water swept through, carrying the massive logs with it.

Filled with horror, Kate reined in Windsong and dropped onto the bridge. But Erik was there first. When he jumped on Dugan's back, the man fell forward onto the gears. As Dugan's face flushed red, the cables stopped turning.

With one quick movement Erik stood up. Leaning forward, he turned the wheel that raised the gate. The rush of water stopped.

Kate breathed a sigh of relief. The great lake filled with logs was again held back by the giant gate.

"Help!" Dugan cried out, still in that strange position on top of the gears.

A grin spread across Erik's face. "Don't you worry!" he told Dugan. "Help is on the way!"

Then Kate saw it—Dugan's necktie caught between the cable and the gear. But would the necktie hold him?

In that moment Kate heard another cry. The voice came from the river.

Kate ran to the railing. On the downstream side of the dam, logs filled the water. The boat Kate had seen lay at a strange angle. The man clung to the sides.

"Help!" he called. "My boat is sinking!"

"Let Frawley drown!" Dugan muttered, still trapped himself.

"I'll get him!" Kate leaped into Windsong's saddle. Not for anything would she stay alone with Dugan. The mare galloped to the end of the bridge. When they reached the Minnesota dike, Kate urged Windsong down the bank into the river.

To Kate's relief the logs had moved beyond them. But now she had a new worry. Could she reach Frawley in time?

I can't lose sight of him, Kate thought, staring ahead. The gatekeeper still clung to the side of the boat, but it was sinking fast. Only a rim of wood showed above the water.

"Help!" he shouted again. "Help!"

22

Someday

"*Hang* on!" Kate called back. Yet she and Windsong were too far upstream. What if they missed Frawley?

At first the water was shallow. Before long it rose around Windsong's legs. When it reached the mare's belly, Kate felt the current with her feet. As the water flowed through a narrow opening in the dam, it rushed downstream. Even a strong swimmer could go down in that.

A scared feeling washed over Kate—a feeling that warned her. The water in Rice Lake had lifted her off Windsong's back. If she, too, was caught in the current, could she hang onto the horse? And could a swimming horse pull both her and Frawley out? Kate didn't know.

Suddenly she reined in. Glancing down, she saw Dugan's coil of rope. *Maybe . . . just maybe.*

Quickly Kate knotted one end of the rope around the saddle horn, then tied a loop in the other end. With all her strength she flung the looped end toward Frawley.

The rope fell short, but the current caught it, bringing the rope close to the gatekeeper. When it was within two or three feet, Frawley reached out and grabbed it.

As Windsong backed out of the water, Frawley hung on until he touched bottom. By the time he and Kate reached shore, Ben and Anders were climbing down the bank. Three or four men were right behind.

Like Erik, Anders threw his arms around Kate. His voice was gruff as he told her, "Well, you're back, so I can tease you again!" But Kate saw the tears in his eyes.

Ben had an even bigger hug for her. "You're a very little girl for a terrible man like Dugan," he said.

"You're a heroine!" Frawley told Kate as soon as he caught his breath. The great rush of logs had slammed against his boat, pushing it into an old log stuck in the river bottom. With the gear weighing down the boat, it didn't take long to sink.

When Kate rode Windsong onto the bridge again, she saw that Erik had tied Dugan's hands and feet. Part of Dugan's necktie was still caught between the cable and the gear.

As Ben searched Dugan, he found the payroll and took it from him. Then Ben and the other men carried Dugan up the road to the office.

There Mr. Frawley clapped Ben on the shoulder and shook the hands of Kate, Anders, and Erik.

"There ought to be something I can give as a reward," he said. "What can I do to thank you?"

"Sir," Kate said softly. She was afraid to tell him, but if she didn't, she'd be giving up Windsong. "There *is* something."

"Yes? What is it?"

"Dugan burned down our barn," Kate said. "Papa is getting wild hay from the meadows. But we're very short of oats. And so is Erik's family."

"You are?" Mr. Frawley looked from one to the other and smiled. "Well, I'm not short of oats. We had rain at just the right time. That's a very fitting reward."

He led them outside. "I'll loan you some harness. If you

hitch up this wagon, we'll fill it with all the oats you can use. And you and Erik can come back for more."

On the way home, Kate, Erik, and Lutfisk rode in the wagon behind Windsong and Breeza.

"I found you! I found you!" Kate kept saying to Windsong. "And I don't have to sell you!"

Each time Kate spoke, the mare's ears turned to the sound of her voice. Windsong seemed just as happy as she was to be together again.

"In my wildest dreams I didn't think this would happen!" Kate said.

"And you even have horses who do tricks!" Anders told her as he rode alongside.

"Wait till I tell Lars!" Kate exclaimed. "He'll teach Breeza how to dance. Next summer Lars and I can ride the horses in Grantsburg's Fourth of July parade!"

When Kate and the others reached home, Papa and Grandpa had come back from the meadows. Large haystacks were drying there, waiting for their return.

Papa was relieved that they had found Windsong. "Does she seem all right?" he asked Kate.

"She acts the same," Kate told him. "But on the way home I noticed that her belly seems more swollen than it was. Does she look all right to you?"

As Papa walked around the horse, he grinned at Anders. Yet when Papa turned back to Kate, she knew he took her question seriously.

"Windsong is fine," he said. "Just fine."

Then Kate told him about Mr. Frawley's reward. "He said we can come back for more oats—enough for Erik's family too."

Papa's grin returned. "Thank you very much!"

A few days later Ben came home, and neighbors gathered together for a barn raising. All day long the men worked hard. One group dropped trees and stripped bark.

Others hewed the logs, then notched and set them in place.

When the walls were high enough to build the floor of the hayloft, men gathered on the west side of the barn. Big Gust lifted the end of a pole about forty feet long. The other men slipped a supporting pole underneath.

While Gust held up the other end of the long pole, men set more poles the entire length of the barn. Soon all the supports were in place and braced.

That night and every night until the work was finished people rolled out their blankets. Women and children slept in the house wherever there was room. Men and older boys slept in the granary and summer kitchen.

When the workers finished the barn, they walked through the woods to Ben's house. Kate followed with coffee.

Big Gust placed a strong pole under the burned corner of the house. While he held up that end, men slipped blocks in place. As soon as the end was braced, they pulled out the charred sections and replaced them with good logs. Then Gust lowered the house in place.

In no time at all, the men cut shingles and laid the roof. When Ben returned to Windy Hill Farm that night, his eyes glowed.

"Come back in two weeks," he told everyone as they left. "Come back for our wedding!"

———

Two days before Ben's wedding, Mama sewed the final button on Kate's dress. After lunch Mama and Grandma and Kate went up to her bedroom. At last she would see the finished dress.

"Close your eyes," Mama said as she dropped the soft folds over Kate's head.

"Keep them closed," Mama added as the dress fell in place. Here and there she smoothed the dress, then slipped the handmade loops over the covered buttons.

"All right," Mama said. "You can look."

When Kate opened her eyes, the first thing she noticed was the length of the dress. It fell about her ankles at just the place where Mama's dresses came.

"That means I'm really grown-up!" Kate exclaimed.

"You're really grown-up," Mama answered. Her smile was soft, and Kate saw tears in her eyes.

Mama led Kate to a mirror on the wall.

"See?" Mama asked. "It *is* just the color of your eyes."

Never had Kate had a dress that was so soft, nor so lovely. But something surprised her even more. In the reflection of the mirror she saw Mama standing on one side of her and Grandma on the other. Again Kate wondered if she would ever be a woman like them.

Then there was something she knew. It was their belief in God that made Mama and Grandma strong. Out of their love for Him came everything else they did.

With surprise Kate realized something. "I look like both of you!"

"Yah," Grandma said. Her smile was proud.

"But how can I?" Kate stared at their reflections. "I'm shorter than you, and each of us has a different color hair."

"It's something more," Mama said, as though she wanted Kate to find out for herself.

"Yes, it is!" Kate caught it now. For the first time she saw herself as a young woman. A young woman who loved fun and good times and puzzling out secrets. A young woman who loved to play the organ and ride Windsong. But also a young woman whose steady gaze reached eagerly into the years ahead.

"I really *am* grown-up!" Kate said, unable to hide her surprise.

"You are lovely, Kate," Mama said. "Best of all, you are lovely on the inside."

"Yah." Grandma's eyes were also bright with tears. "You are *God's* young woman."

Once more Kate looked in the mirror. Then she unbraided her hair. As Mama and Grandma watched, Kate brushed her hair upward and practiced pinning it on top of her head. Then they quietly slipped from the room.

———

The morning of Ben's wedding Kate was up early, but Papa had been up earlier still. When he came to the house, he told Kate, "There's something I want you to see in the barn."

Kate's stomach fluttered. Had something else happened? Something bad?

Yet Papa's eyes told her that whatever it was, it was good.

When Kate reached the stall, Windsong lifted her head in greeting. As Kate reached out her hand to stroke the mare's nose, she looked down.

In the fresh straw at Windsong's feet lay a newly born foal.

"It's a filly!" Papa said.

The foal was still wet and as black as Windsong. In the midst of her black was a white snip on her nose and a white blaze on her forehead.

"Ohhhh." Tears blurred Kate's sight. "Windsong had to be carrying the foal when I bought her!"

Papa grinned. "She was so thin it didn't show till you brought her home from Nevers."

"You knew?" Kate asked.

Papa nodded. "I didn't want to get your hopes up in case something went wrong."

Moving quietly to not frighten the foal, Kate knelt down in the straw. With a gentle hand she reached out.

Awkwardly the little filly struggled to her feet. With her long, thin legs spread far apart, she seemed all head and eyes. On wobbly legs she took a step toward Kate.

In that moment Kate knew the foal was hers—really hers!

———

Later that morning, Papa, Anders, and Lars set up saw-horses and placed boards over them to make tables. Soon after Kate covered the boards with tablecloths, people started to come. Kate hurried into the house to put on her new dress. At the last minute she braided her hair, instead of pinning it up.

By noon when everyone had gathered for the wedding, the sky was as blue as Kate's dress. Anders played the fiddle and Erik the guitar. Standing beneath a scarlet maple, Ben and Jenny said "I do."

To Kate the wedding barely seemed real. Then she heard Pastor Munson's words. "What God hath joined together, let no man put asunder."

From where she stood as a bridesmaid, Kate watched Ben slip the ring on Jenny's finger. *Forever,* Kate thought. *Until death parts them.*

In that moment the bigness of marriage struck Kate. As the last words were spoken, she felt overwhelmed by the seriousness of it.

"I now pronounce you man and wife," the pastor said.

As Ben and Jenny turned to face their families and friends, Ben looked down at his new bride.

Kate caught her breath. *Will Erik ever look at me the way Ben looks at Jenny?*

"Well, Kate," Anders said at the reception afterwards. "When do you think you'll get married?"

"Me?" Kate asked. "I haven't the slightest idea."

"C'mon," Anders answered. "Who do you think you're kidding? I'm your brother, remember?"

"And I'm your sister—for a year and a half now. Hasn't it been awful?"

"Well, I don't know." Anders shrugged, as though not wanting to admit too much. "Do you realize all the things we've done together?"

Kate grinned. "Yah sure, you betcha. Remember how I

thought you were a country bumpkin?"

Anders scowled. "I wondered what kind of sister you'd be."

"I wondered what kind of brother you'd be. I sure found out!"

"We've had some hard times," Anders said. "But some good times too. I guess I'm glad you're my sister."

"You are? That's really big praise. I guess I'm glad you're my brother. In fact, I've started to like you."

"Aw, Kate!" Anders flushed deep red. He glanced around, as though hoping no one had heard. "Don't talk that way!"

Kate giggled. "I mean it!"

"Well, there's something I mean," Anders said. "Do you know what I think? I think that someday you and Erik will get married."

Kate's heart leaped, but she tried to pretend her brother's words didn't matter. "What else is going on in that head of yours?"

Anders grinned. "That's for me to know and you to find out."

"Well, if you'll excuse me," Kate said stiffly out of her newfound grown-upness, "I have more immediate things to attend to."

"Like what?" Anders asked.

"Like pouring coffee." Kate hurried into the summer kitchen, found the coffeepot she needed, then returned outside. As she moved through the crowd, her eyes looked for one person.

Finally she saw him, off to one side. Leaning against a tree, Erik was talking to Ben.

Erik really is a special friend, Kate thought. *And yes, he has all the qualities I want in the man I marry. But for now I want to learn how to be a good friend.*

In that moment Erik looked up. As he glanced around, he, too, seemed to be searching for someone.

From across the lawn their gaze met. Erik smiled, and Kate smiled back.

Someday, she thought as she flipped her braid over her shoulder. *Maybe someday.*

Acknowledgments

$\mathcal{O}$ften readers ask me, "Was there really a Big Gust? Was he truly seven-feet, six-inches tall?

Yes, there really was a Big Gust, and he was loved by young and old. Not only was he Grantsburg's village marshall for nearly a quarter of a century, but also captain of the fire department, a lamplighter, road surveyor, and charter member of the English Lutheran Church. The stories I tell about him are either true or consistent with things he was known to do.

If you visit northwest Wisconsin and the village of Grantsburg, you will see a life-sized wooden carving of Big Gust. In the Grantsburg Historical Society Museum, you'll find his uniform and crutch. His grave in Riverside Cemetery is simply marked *Big Gust*.

In this novel, as in others where this much-loved hero takes part, I was helped by Mildred Hedlund and by Eunice Kanne's book *Big Gust: Grantsburg's Legendary Giant*.

Electric lights, which were new to the country in 1889, were used in the twenty-four-hour-a-day construction of

Nevers Dam. Sightseers came from miles around to view "the lights that never went out."

When the eighty-foot Lang gate (also known as the big bear trap) was open, eight million board feet of timber could pass through in two hours. The logs sluiced through Nevers Dam during its lifetime could have built approximately 920,000 homes.

The Nevers Dam site is now part of the Wild River State Park at Center City, Minnesota. Dave Crawford, park naturalist, was extremely helpful to me in writing this book.

Throughout this series, Walter and Ella Johnson have given me much-needed information. I am also indebted to Dale Dahl, former fire chief of the Grantsburg Fire Department, and to Judy Pearson and other members of the Grantsburg Historical Society. Berdella Johnson, Alton Jensen, and Clarence Wagman gave special assistance regarding Charlie Saunders' livery stable.

Thanks to many other Grantsburg area residents: Clayton Jorgenson, Betty Peer, Maurice and Arleth Erickson, Sheila Meyer, Kelly Johnson, Mary Hedlund-Blomberg, Jim Glover, Patty Meyer, Raymond (Bob) Johnson, Janet Hartzell, and the librarians at the Grantsburg Public Library.

My gratitude also to the *Inter-County Leader* for the newspaper article from the Frederic *Star*, to Leigh and Joyce Wold, Cliff Bjork, Mildred Hartshorn, Dr. N. E. Olson, Lois and Dick Klawitter, Randy and Renee Klawitter, Dorothy Langstaff, and Fred Dahlinger, Jr., Director of the Robert L. Parkinson Library and Research Center at Circus World, Baraboo, Wisconsin.

Wade Brask answered countless questions about early Wisconsin farm life and the Windy Hill Farm site. Diane Brask shared her love for and experience with horses and gave time to read and comment on the manuscript. John Daniel Draper of Bethany, West Virginia, gave excellent suggestions for writing about specially trained horses.

Ron Klug helped in the development and editing of each book in the series. Thanks, Ron! And thanks to the entire

Bethany team, and especially my editors, Barbara Lilland, Doris Holmlund, and Helen Motter. As always, my big, big appreciation for my husband, Roy, and his ongoing encouragement.

Finally, my gratitude to all of the people of northwest Wisconsin. When we moved to the area, I had no idea I would write a series. Then I learned that many of you have been friends and neighbors for three and four generations. You told me stories that were too good to be lost. You helped me value the way of life you have known, as well as your integrity, love, and courage. Thank you for letting Roy and me become part of your lives.

You who are readers have often asked me, "Do the Northwoods books come out of your own life?" Though each novel is definitely fiction, my experiences have influenced what I write.

Before our marriage, my husband, Roy, was a widower, his first wife dying when he was twenty-seven. When we were married two years later, Roy's daughter, Gail, was our flower girl. In time, two additional children, Jeffrey and Kevin, were born and grew tall like Anders and Erik. Now, all of our children have families of their own. Our youngest son is also a writer, the author of such books as *Can I Be a Christian Without Being Weird?*

Just like Kate, Roy and I knew and loved Minneapolis before moving to northwest Wisconsin. Within the novels there are "secrets" that reflect both my family and his. We are still close to the immigrant heritage that made America strong.

As a young woman, Roy's mother immigrated from Norway. In a wave of homesickness she had her picture taken and sent back to her family. The result was the family picture described in *The Disappearing Stranger* and other books that follow. Roy's father also immigrated from Norway, and the two met in Milwaukee.

Carl Nordstrom is named after two more immigrants— my Swedish grandfather, Carl Johnson, and my Swedish grandmother, Mathilda, whose maiden name was Nordstrom. While a young woman, Grandma worked on a farm outside Walnut Grove, Minnesota, and often watched wagon trains pass through to settle in the West.

When Grandpa and Grandma Johnson were married, they bought a farm on the banks of Plum Creek. My father grew up there, and many of the stories about runaway horses come out of his experience in riding and breaking broncos.

Years later, during summer vacations, my sisters and I often played in Plum Creek. From where we waded, the water flowed under a bridge into the land once owned by the family of Laura Ingalls Wilder.

Apparently Grandma Johnson had great plans for my father, for she gave him a long name—*Alvar Bernhard Walfrid Johnson*. While a young man, he dropped the Johnson because of the great number of people with that name. As a result, I grew up a Walfrid, then married a Johnson! However, we are not related to the Walfrid Johnson in the novels.

The ADVENTURES OF THE NORTHWOODS series also reflects the Danish side of my family, though in a more hidden way. When my Danish grandfather came to America, he worked for about a year to save enough money to bring my grandmother and their three-year-old daughter, Lydia, across the Atlantic. While passing through Ellis Island, Grandma and Lydia had pieces of paper pinned on their coats, as described in *Grandpa's Stolen Treasure*.

That novel pictures my Danish grandparents as they looked when I was a child. A few months after the book was published, I learned that when Grandma came to Rochester, Minnesota, as an immigrant, there was a mix-up at the depot. Grandpa "lost" her and Lydia for an entire day!

As you might guess, three-year-old Lydia grew up to be my mother.

Some of the Spirit Lake School experiences come out of my own childhood. I attended my first four grades in a two-room country school on the shores of Goose Lake, near

Scandia, Minnesota. Miss Sundquist gives spelling words exactly as my teacher, Miss Guslander, did. There were drafts through the knotholes in the floor at Goose Lake, too, as well as box socials, a woodshed, and a large wood stove. Even as a child, I knew it was special to attend a school surrounded by woods and water.

And yes, there's something else. While a beekeeper, I, too, have known what it means to have a bear tear open my hives.

However, the most important reflection of our personal lives is shown in the life of faith the Windy Hill family walks. Both Roy and I value the privilege of being brought up in that kind of home. It is deeply moving to us to know that over one hundred years ago our relatives read the same Bible verses we now read. The winds of time have brought countless changes, but God is the same. So is His message of hope and love and forgiveness.

During the life of this series, many of you have written, saying, "Please, please, don't ever stop writing the Northwoods books!" I'm grateful that you feel that way. I have enjoyed finding out what Kate and Anders and Erik will do, in the same way that you have liked reading about them. Yet, as I begin a different series, there are some things you can do.

One of them is to read back over the Northwoods books. Start at the beginning with *The Disappearing Stranger* and read the books in the order in which they were written. You'll get to know Kate and her friends even better. Perhaps you'll want to make up your own stories about the Windy Hill family.

You can also join me in something new—the RIVERBOAT ADVENTURES series. You may find that the kids in this series remind you of Kate and Anders, Lars, Erik, and Josie. They'll have some of the same problems, as well as the same fun. They'll be curious, solve mysteries, and meet danger in the same way as the Northwoods family. They'll be like kids you know, and maybe just like you.

Instead of a farm, Libby and her friends will live on a riverboat. As they travel about, they may visit your town or city.

Listen! Can you hear the whistle? There's a steamboat a-comin'!